Cora

The Brides of San Francisco 3

CYNTHIA WOOLF

DEDICATION

For Jim. Thank you for putting me to bed all those nights I fell asleep at my desk. Thank you for being my greatest cheerleader.

I love you so much.

ACKNOWLEDGMENTS

For my Just Write partners Michele Callahan, Karen Docter, and Cate Rowan, thank you for brainstorming with me when I'm stuck and getting me to write the next one.

For my wonderful cover artist, Romcon Custom Covers. Thank you for the most beautiful covers ever.

For my wonderful editor, Linda Carroll-Bradd, you make my stories so much better.

CHAPTER 1

Monday, March 25, 1867
New York City

Cora Jones stood outside the office of Matchmaker & Co., tugging at her cuffs, pulling them down over the top of her gloves. Her yellow walking dress was the latest fashion with a wide-sleeved short jacket over a dress with long tight sleeves. Naturally wide hips caused Cora to eschew a crinoline in favor of several petticoats to achieve the wide, full skirt she wanted. Short and round, not the easiest to fit, she was proud of her skills as a seamstress. She stood straight, hoping to seem taller than her five-foot-two inch stature.

Passersby looked at her askance but she ignored them while she prepared herself to enter.

The building looked exactly like every other building on the block. Three story, red brick with two windows on each floor facing the street. The only difference was the color of the doors. The other buildings had somber dark brown doors. Her building had a bright blue door.

When she was certain she looked her best she opened the cheerful blue door and entered. She was at this office today to pick up her ticket for passage aboard the Southern Star to San Francisco to meet her future husband, Harry Belcher.

She'd been corresponding with Harry for a year. She still remembered the day Mrs. Maggie Selby, proprietress of Matchmaker & Co. had shown her the pictures of potential husbands. All of them were good looking men. All were financially stable. She'd chosen Harry because he appeared to her to be kind, with his blond hair and round face.

"Ah, Miss Jones. So good to see you. Sit down. Please." She pointed at the chair in front of the desk. "Three brides will be aboard the Southern Star this trip. You, Nellie Wallace with her two children and a maid, and Annie Markum. Annie is the youngest of you, only twenty-two."

"That's not so young. Only four years younger than me. Not really much in the scheme of things."

"Quite true. Now, here is your travel voucher. The ship sails with the tide on the first of April. Be at Pier Six at eight in the morning to get settled aboard."

Cora folded the paper and placed it safely in her reticule. The document was the ticket to her future and worth her weight in gold. Gaining her own husband and children were the possibilities at the other end— something she'd never thought she'd have since her fiancé, Asa Woods, died during the last battle of the War Between the States.

She stood and smoothed her skirt preparing to leave.

Maggie Selby came around to the front of the desk. "I'll miss your skills, Miss Jones. You're the most talented of all Madam Duval's seamstresses. From now on my dresses will never be as nice as the ones you made for me."

CYNTHIA WOOLF

"Thank you for saying so, Mrs. Selby. I shall keep up my skills in San Francisco. I'm taking three steamer trunks full of bolts of cloth, sewing notions and several pattern books. Depending on how things work out, I may open my own dress shop…if my new husband doesn't mind, plus I plan to make my own clothes."

Maggie shook her head. "You won't need to do either once you're married to Harry Belcher. He's quite wealthy. He started the San Francisco Bank and Trust and is the company's president."

"I know. He's been sure to inform me of his wealth and that I won't have to work, but once he sees me, he may not want to marry me and I need to have something to fall back on." Cora was happy she wouldn't have to work to support herself. Starting a business was a thrilling and risky proposition. Being able to do it and not have to worry about making a living with it was a luxury she was grateful for.

Mrs. Selby frowned. "Why wouldn't he want to marry you?"

Cora could tell by Mrs. Selby's expression that she really had no idea why a man wouldn't want to marry her.

"I'm plump. Round. My mother called me sturdy. However you say the words, they mean the same thing. I'm fat and unfashionable right now. On top of that I'm short." She waved her hand up and down her length.

"But, I do make an effort. I sew all my own clothes, so I can be in fashionable styles that fit me. I can practically adjust patterns in my sleep. Well, thank you for everything. I must go home and start packing. I've only got a week and lots to do."

"Of course." Maggie Selby came forward and gave Cora a hug. "Have a wonderful life, Miss Jones."

"Thank you. I intend to."

*****

Cora was the last of the brides to arrive at the pier. She had five trunks to oversee. One with her clothes, three filled to the brim with bolts of cloth and sewing accessories. The last one was her hope chest with her linens and her mother's china, some baby clothes she'd made, and other things she would need for married life.

Her brother, Virgil, had no interest in any of her mother's things except the house on Long Island. And in the end, after Virgil was killed, even that had come to Cora. She'd sold her home and everything else except these five trunks and had quite a tidy sum with which to open her shop. Harry wouldn't have to help her with the finances of the business at all. Her wealth would give her the independence she'd grown accustomed to.

She'd become a mail-order bride initially because of the lack of marriageable men in New York due to the war. Now she found she was thrilled at the thought of the adventure that awaited her.

The cab dropped her and her trunks at the end of Pier Six where the Southern Star waited. The boat was a large passenger ship, purportedly capable of transporting sixty people, plus the crew. The captain stood on the dock checking in the passengers, and several sailors waited nearby for loading the baggage.

A tall, blonde woman with two children approached Cora. Well, tall by Cora's standards, she was probably only about five feet, seven inches tall.

"Hello, I'm Nellie Wallace. Are you a bride from Matchmaker & Co.?"

"Yes, I'm Cora Jones. Nice to meet you." She extended her hand.

Nellie shook her hand. "Those are my little darlings, Henry and Violet." She pointed at a young boy and toddler girl playing nearby. "Henry is keeping Violet occupied. She's quite the busy bee, otherwise."

"Oh, thank goodness," said a young redheaded woman standing nearby. "I couldn't help but overhear that you're from Matchmaker & Co. Me, too. I'm Annie Markum and I'm so pleased to make your acquaintances."

"Hello, I'm Cora Jones and this is Nellie Wallace."

"Ladies," said the captain. "Time to board."

With little fuss, Cora and the others found their rooms. Nellie and the children had a cabin to themselves, while Cora and Annie shared accommodations. Other than the captain's quarters, these were the only private cabins on board. Everyone else slept in steerage, in bunks that were barely wide enough to house one person and were only about five feet long. Lord help you if you were a tall man.

Over the course of the trip, all three women became close friends. Cora taught the other two how to sew which came in handy for Nellie. Since Henry grew so quickly, his pants had to be let down in length while they were on board.

*****

San Francisco, California
June 2, 1867

The ship arrived after hitting bad weather for just two days during the entire trip. They'd had one day with no wind at all and another that was almost a hurricane, the winds were so strong. The captain said the weather on a trip like theirs always varied. He was grateful they had mostly fair days which had resulted in a very good trip during which they'd made good time. They actually arrived three days sooner than they'd expected to.

As soon as they disembarked in San Francisco, they were whisked away by horse-drawn cabs, to the Golden State Hotel where Mrs. Selby had arranged for them to stay for up to two months. She wanted the women to get to know the men they were to marry and not be rushed into a quick wedding.

The inside of the hotel was not something Cora would ever have dreamed of seeing. The walls were white, the carpets and furniture all varying shades of red. The result was generally gaudy but the place was clean and seemed to be well kept.

Cora checked in and found a message waiting from Harry Belcher.

My dear Cora,

I have instructed the staff at the hotel to send a messenger to me when you get there. I should be arriving shortly after that as my bank is only minutes away. I am most anxious to greet you in person.

Yours truly,

Harry Belcher

Cora read the missive and smiled. After a year of correspondence, it seemed so like Harry to come to greet her right away.

"Cora?"

A deep, familiar voice came from behind her. But that was impossible...she slowly turned toward the sound.

"Cora. It's me."

"Asa?" Cora gasped and placed a hand

on her chest. She shook her head slowly. It couldn't be. Asa was dead. They'd told her he died at Appomattox more than two years ago. Her eyes filled with tears. "No. No. You're dead."

He held his hat in his hands, rolling the brim and crushing the felt between his fingers. His black suit and tie fit him well and his tanned skin was stark against the white of his shirt. She remembered his beautiful blue eyes, but the gray in his brown hair was new.

"I wanted you to think that. I was wounded and I…"

He took a halting step toward her.

She saw his limp and stepped back, eyes wide. "Asa, I—"

"Cora Jones?"

Another male voice called her name from across the hotel lobby.

She looked up and saw Harry Belcher crossing the room toward her. Her breath hitched and she smiled. Just like the picture he'd sent, he had blond hair, parted in the middle and slicked down. She knew from her correspondence with him that his eyes were green. The tan three-piece suit with brown tie and top hat would have washed out his pale skin, but the blue shirt he wore added color to his face.

"Cora, I've come home to you," said Asa.

How could he be coming home to her when they were on the opposite side of the country from where they'd lived? How did he find her?

Harry reached them and took Cora's hand, brought it to his lips and kissed the top. "You're as beautiful as your picture, and such a tiny little thing." He reached out a hand toward her.

"Harry, I—"

"Cora, I know you came here to be a bride, but since I'm back," said Asa. "You belong to me."

"What does he mean, you belong to him?" Harry frowned and pointed at Asa. "Who is this man? What does his being here have to do with anything? You're going to marry me. We have a contract."

"Asa is my fiancé but he was supposed to be dead." She looked back and forth between Asa and Harry and then burst into tears.

"Cora, are you all right?" Nellie called on her way to her room.

"Yes, I'll be fine," said Cora, sniffling.

Nellie nodded and went on her way.

Cora turned back to the two men, both vying for her attention and each demanding that she marry him.

With a shaky hand, she took a hanky from her reticule and dabbed at her eyes. "Asa, I have no idea what you're doing here, but after two years, you cannot really believe you have any hold upon me. You could have contacted me anytime in those years but you didn't."

She turned to the other man. "Harry we do have a contract, but that was when I thought myself an unattached woman. With Asa back I must give all of this more thought. I have two months here at the hotel and I won't be bullied by either of you into making a decision right this second."

"Well, I never," huffed Harry.

Asa looked smug and Cora wanted to wipe that look off his face.

She narrowed her eyes and stared at them both. "You'll have to convince me before I'll marry either one of you. In other words you're both going to have to court me. I'll make my decision within the next two months. And let me warn you, I may decide not to marry either of you. Right now, neither of you is showing me your best side."

"Well, I *want* to court you." Asa's blue eyes echoed his sincerity. "I didn't have time before I went into the army. I want to prove to you I'm the man you should marry."

"I'll be the man you choose. I've never lost something important to me and you, Cora," Harry looked her straight in the eyes, his green ones meeting with her brown ones, "are important to me."

The look Harry gave her was one of determination and she liked that very much. "Very good. We'll start tonight. One of you will take me to dinner. I've got a number in my mind. The one of you closest to the number may escort me to dinner this evening."

"Six," said Asa.

"Five," said Harry.

"The number is seven. Asa it is. Pick me up here at seven o'clock." Cora turned on her heel and walked toward the stairs to her room.

Asa crossed his arms, smiled and watched her walk away. "She's the same as

I remember. So full of fire. Ready for an adventure."

"I'm going to win her," said Harry. "I never lose."

"Prepare to lose this time. I've loved Cora all my life and won't be losing her to you."

Harry snorted. "If you really loved her, you wouldn't have disappeared from her life for so long." He adjusted his jacket, turned and left the hotel.

That stung, and Asa knew the boastful man was right, but he'd been scared. He'd awakened in a field hospital minus his left leg below the knee. His immediate thoughts were he wanted to die because he was no longer a man.

There had been a brilliant young doctor, Matthew Reynolds, who wouldn't let him die. He worked with him, got him up and walking. Made him believe there was something to live for. Something more than just his work as a newspaper reporter, though since Aunt Charlotte's death, he didn't need to work ever again. He'd have to manage the investments, but that was hardly full time work.

But he'd been afraid Cora would reject

him. Rather than give her the chance to choose, he stayed away. Doctor Reynolds finally convinced him to give her the benefit of the doubt and let her know he was alive. Convinced him to let her have the choice and to be prepared if she felt the loss of his leg was something she could not cope with.

He'd returned to New York, to her house and found the building locked up, sold and Cora gone. He found out about her becoming a bride and went to Matchmaker & Co to talk to the owner, Mrs. Margaret Selby. She'd made him explain everything; including admitting that he loved Cora, before she would tell him where Cora was.

"You're too late, sir." Mrs. Selby said finally. "She sailed for San Francisco two days ago with the tide."

"I'll go overland. It's the only chance I have of getting there before her. It should only take a month and sailing will take at least two. I'll still have to convince her to marry me, but I love her too much not to try."

Mrs. Selby sighed. "I shouldn't be telling you this, but she mentioned you and I do believe you love her. Love is one of the reasons I'm in this business. I want these women to find love, but be safe while doing it. Only because I can tell you love Cora and she was unaware of your existence, am I'm telling you. She needs to know. She needs to be given the choice. So, she'll be at the Golden State Hotel. She's set to be there for two months after they arrive in San Francisco. After that you're on your own."

Asa took her hand in both of his and shook it. "Thank you, Mrs. Selby. I'll repay you whatever you might be out for Cora's match."

"Don't be so sure she won't have gone ahead and married before you arrive. The hotel is guaranteed for two months but people have been known to wed quickly."

"I'll get there and she won't have married. I have to believe that. I can't lose her again."

"Then I suggest you get going and catch that train as soon as you can."

He nodded and smiled. "Yes, ma'am."

The trip would be hard and would take nearly a month, but hard or not, it was worth it if he got to San Francisco before Cora.

CHAPTER 2

Cora dressed with care in her most demure evening dress. Made out of brown satin, the gown looked wonderful with her dark brown hair and coppery eyes. She also wore a brown and blue paisley shawl to ward off the chill night air. Though San Francisco was generally warmer than New York, and at least snow didn't happen here, the city sat directly on the bay and the breezes off the ocean kept the temperature cool, especially at night.

At fifteen minutes before seven o'clock that evening, Cora walked down the stairs to the lobby. She thought she'd have to wait for Asa, but he was already there sitting on one of the chairs. When he saw her, he stood and walked toward her. He looked handsome, still wearing the same black suit he had earlier in the day, but somehow he seemed broader of shoulder and slimmer of waist. He had a definite limp.

"Cora," he said, stopping in front of her. "Thank you for choosing me to take you to dinner tonight."

She shook her head. "I had nothing to do with it. You simply were nearest the number I'd chosen. If you think I planned it that way, you are mistaken. Don't think I'll be easy on you, Asa."

He reddened around the ears and slightly ducked his head. "You're right. I don't deserve any special preference."

"And you'll get none from me. As far as I'm concerned, you deserted me." Her anger and hurt seemed as fresh as it had when she'd first been notified of his death. "You let me believe you were dead for two years. Don't expect to just fall back in where we were." She furrowed her brows. "It's not going to happen. You'll have to convince me you're the man I should choose."

"I understand. You must be angry with me."

"You know *nothing* of my anger. Did you know Virgil died at Gettysburg?" She twisted the strings of her reticule. "I've been taking care of myself for a long time, Asa. Don't think you can waltz back into my life and just take over. I won't have it."

"I don't want to take over, and I don't want to fight." He ran a hand through his hair. "We have a lot of catching up to do. Can't we just start there, like we are just getting to know one another for the first time? In a way we are because neither of us is the same person we were before I left for the war so many years ago."

"You're right. We've both changed over the years, and I mean more than just physically." Done with that conversation, she steered it to a safer subject. "Where would you like to go? We can eat here in the hotel restaurant. That might be the best choice for our first night, since neither of us knows much about the city yet."

"That's fine with me. I'll get to spend more time with you that way. Tomorrow I'll scout for a new place to take you next time."

Cora was pleased. He would try to make an effort. That was a good start to their new relationship.

They went to the restaurant and were seated almost immediately. The establishment was more elegant than Cora could have imagined considering the décor of the lobby. The tables, seating either two or four, were covered in bright white linen with napkins of dark blue, contrasting nicely against the tablecloth. The walls were papered in lovely light blue and green stripes, with pictures of seas and forests on alternating panels. There was none of the garish red of the lobby.

The waiter brought menus and glasses of water. "I'll give you a few minutes to look over the selections," said the young man. "The chef's special is baked swordfish with a lemon-butter sauce, served with new red potatoes and asparagus. We also have fresh apple pie for dessert."

After the server departed, Cora said, "That all sounds good to me. I think I'll have the special."

"We'll make it two."

Cora shook out her napkin and placed it in her lap, more for something to do than out of necessity. "Why did you let me believe you were dead? How could you do that to me?" she asked softly over the lump in her throat. All the hurt she felt came out in those words. She'd never been madly in love with Asa, but she had cared deeply for him, and the fact he let her grieve over him wounded her.

He placed his hands, one on top of the other, on the table. "I was afraid," he slowly admitted.

"Of what?"

He didn't look at her, but looked down at his hands. "That since I only have one leg now, you'd think me less than a man. I considered myself less than whole, how could you not?"

"Why would you think that? You should have let me make that decision." She reached across the table and placed her hand atop his. "I would never have thought less of you. Men came home from the war with all kinds of wounds. None of them are less a man because of them. They are heroes, each and every one, just as you are."

He shook his head. "I got hit with a cannon ball. I'm not a hero."

Cora squeezed his hand. "You went to war. You fought for your country. That makes you a hero in my book."

He slowly lifted his head until his gaze

met hers. "Really? You feel that way?"

She nodded. "Yes, I do. I always have and if you really knew me, you'd have known that. Our problem was we didn't know each other. Otherwise you'd never have thought that way of me. You were Virgil's best friend. Though I was acquainted with you, you knew my brother, not me. I just tagged along."

Asa nodded. "I suppose that's true."

She took a sip of water. Her throat was dry and the words were hard to utter. "Why did you ask me to marry you?"

He stacked his fork on his knife and then unstacked them before answering. "I wanted someone waiting for me when I came home. I wanted to know that someone cared."

"Well," she swallowed the lump in her throat. "I did. And now I find you betrayed me. Betrayed the trust I had in you. How can you expect me to ever trust you again?"

"I'm so sorry, Cora. I never intended to hurt you, simply to protect myself. Let me prove myself to you. Let me earn your trust."

Before she could answer the waiter came back to the table and took their order. After he left, Cora asked, "I was too flustered to ask before, but how did you find me? And how did you make it to San Francisco before I did?"

He took a sip of water. "You're old neighbor, Mrs. Boyle told me you'd become a bride and gave me Mrs. Selby's direction. I went to see her and she gave me this hotel's name. As to how we arrived before you, I took the train to Missouri and the stagecoach from there to San Francisco. I arrived a couple of weeks ago. It took me about a month of hard travel, but it was worth it. You're worth everything to me."

She cocked her head. "So you just staked out the lobby until I showed up? What if we hadn't arrived until mid June, which was our original arrival date?"

He shrugged. "I'd have stayed. I'll do whatever it takes. When I got here I took a room so they wouldn't throw me out if I sat down and waited in the lobby for you to get here. What room are you in? I'm in 203."

"They put all of us, the brides I mean, on the fifth floor."

"How many brides are there?"

"Just three. Me, Nellie Wallace who has two children and a servant with her, and Annie Markum."

"I didn't realize that women with children became brides."

"More often than you might think. When the men came back from the war, they were able to pick and choose women for their wives, widows with children were not as in demand. Most men want to have their own children. They don't want to raise someone else's. But with Nellie, she was leaving an intolerable situation, living with her in-laws. She became a bride to escape that. To give her children a fighting chance to not become terrible people like their father and her in-laws"

"I see. I hadn't thought of that, but I suppose that would be true. Unless I was madly in love, I probably wouldn't want to marry a woman with children either."

"See? You think like most men. Out west, men want wives, helpmates and children are not seen as much of a detriment as they are back home."

Their supper came and conversation stopped for a time. Cora was not a delicate eater. She had an appetite for food and for life. Neither of which she denied nor apologized for.

"Do you remember when we went for a

hike in the woods behind the house?" She smiled at the memory. "You and Virgil were so mean. You'd get ahead of me and then jump out at me as I passed."

He laughed. "And you would scream and jump every time."

"Ah, but did you know that I was faking it?" She grinned wider. "I knew where you were every time. You two didn't hide very well, but I figured as long as you both could laugh with me along, then you'd let me keep tagging along with you."

"I never minded you coming with us. Virgil on the other hand, found it inconvenient to have you along when all he wanted to do was meet girls."

"You both had plenty of girls chasing after you." She lifted her chin at him. "You especially, if I remember correctly, had plenty of pretty girls hanging around. I was a little jealous of them as I got older."

She took another bit of her dinner. "I can't believe how wonderful the food is here. When I first came in and saw the red décor in the lobby, I was taken aback. I admit I was concerned about the rooms. But everything I've seen, except the lobby, is tastefully decorated."

"It is. And the lobby has grown on me. Sitting in there for the days on end, I've gotten used to the color. It's not so bad."

She shuddered and shook her head. "I don't think I could ever get used the gaudiness of the room."

After dinner, she and Asa walked back to her room. She was careful to walk slower than she might have otherwise, but not by much. Asa was very good with his leg.

"I had a nice evening. Thank you for dinner." She reached into her reticule for her key.

"You're welcome." He smiled and gave her a little half bow. "I hope we'll go again day after tomorrow. I'd like to take you on a picnic and maybe we can see some of the sights together."

She smiled. "I'd like that."

Asa lifted her hand to his lips and gently kissed the top. "Until then." He turned and walked down the hall, back toward the staircase.

Cora went into her room and shut the door behind her, then leaned back against it, her heart lighter than it had been in a long time. Light from the window illuminated her way and she moved to the bedside table. She struck a wooden match and lit the lamp, setting on the nightstand. As she blew out the match, her thoughts returned to her evening with Asa. She had a wonderful night. Even though they had a long way to go, he hadn't hedged when she asked the hard questions. He admitted his mistake and that, in her mind, allowed them to start over.

She took off her gloves and put them, along with her reticule, on the top of the bureau. Then she undressed, laying her dress and petticoats on the end of the bed. She put her corset on the top of the bureau with her gloves. Keeping on her pantaloons she put on her nightgown and robe. Then she poured water from the pitcher into the basin and washed her face and hands.

On one side of the room was a small table with two chairs. She took the lamp and set it on the table while she opened one of her trunks and found her diary.

June 2, 1867
Dear Diary,
I had dinner with Asa tonight. All this time, I had thought him dead. I still have a problem with finding out he let me think that rather than face me with only one leg. He

was too afraid of how I would react to the fact he lost his leg. I wish he'd known me better, trusted me not to hurt him. I would never have thought less of him. Don't think less of him now.

I wonder what he's been doing all this time. He was a newspaper reporter before the war. Was he still able to do that for a living? Or did having only one leg hinder him in that endeavor?

I find that I'm quite attracted to Asa, even after not seeing him for six years. The attraction I felt before was the reason I agreed to marry him in the first place. I'll have a very difficult time making a decision between Harry and Asa. The Harry I know from his letters is also a very nice man and he is certainly handsome.

I've decided to open a dress shop right away. I have to find rental space for the store and will ask Nellie's husband, Blake Malone, to help me find an appropriate location for the store. Nellie and Annie and I became so close on the trip here. They are truly my best friends, sisters of my heart, besides being the only ones that I know here in San Francisco.

Blake is a self made man according to

Nellie. With his knowledge of the city, I believe he'll be able to help me find a place for my business. She trusts him enough to marry him, I guess I can trust him to find rental space for my shop.

I wasn't going to open the dress shop so soon, but with this quandary I'm in, trying to decide between Harry and Asa, I've decided I need to move forward with those plans. I wonder how Harry or Asa will feel about his wife, assuming I marry one of them, opening a business. Mrs. Selby said I wouldn't need to support myself if I marry Harry because he's a wealthy man, but I want to know that I can provide for myself if I need to. Besides, I like sewing clothes and making people feel good about themselves.

Tomorrow is dinner with Harry. The difference between the two men will be interesting to see. After all Harry lives here and will be able to take me to a nice restaurant. Perhaps one that overlooks the bay or up on one of the hills.

We'll just have to wait and see what happens. Goodnight, Dear Diary. I'll be back tomorrow night with more adventures.

*****

Harry knocked on Cora's door at six-thirty in the evening.

"Mr. Belcher. Right on time. Let me get my shawl."

"Please, my dear, call me Harry."

"And you may call me Cora."

"It will be my pleasure. We've been corresponding for long enough, that I feel like we know each other very well."

Eight letters over the period of a year, was not what she called very well.

She'd unpacked her trunk in anticipation of a long stay at the hotel. Tonight she wore a modest gown of brown and gold striped silk. Cora generally wasn't a fan of stripes especially horizontal ones but the pattern was in such fashion now, she decided she needed at least one dress in that material.

The brown and gold, small vertical stripe was the least offensive that she could find and she'd designed the dress so it actually flattered her figure. She'd cut the material on the bias for the top, slanting the stripes from her shoulders to the middle of her waist and left the stripe going up and down on the skirt. This made her waist seem extra small. She'd received many compliments on the dress.

Cora grabbed her reticule, black gloves and shawl, and then went to the door where Harry waited.

"I'm ready."

"You look lovely tonight, Cora."

"Thank you. You look rather fine yourself."

He did, too. Harry wore a dark brown suit with knee length cutaway coat and white shirt with brown tie. He carried a black top hat.

Cora tucked her hand through the crook of his offered arm.

"I thought I'd take you to one of my favorite restaurants. They serve the freshest fish in the city."

"I'd like that. Fish is one of my favorite foods. I had swordfish last night that was very good."

"That's right you had dinner with *him* last night."

"Harry, he has a name. Asa. And if nothing else, he is my friend. I'd appreciate if you would remember that."

"I'm sorry, m'dear, I guess I'm letting my jealousy show. I'm still a little upset that you are considering this man's suit at all."

She let go of his arm taking hold of the

banister to descend the staircase. "I don't see how I cannot. I was engaged to him and would never have contracted to be a mail-order bride had I known he was alive. Because I didn't know, I accepted your contract. If you would rather, I'll repay you for the voyage and for this hotel and we can forget this happened."

Wide-eyed at her suggestion, he held up his hands. "No, no I wouldn't rather. I'm quite serious about marrying you. I enjoyed our correspondence and I believe we will be a good match."

"I believe that, too, Harry, or I wouldn't have come. That is why this whole situation is so difficult. You see, I feel the same way about Asa, and we have a history which you and I do not." *This is so difficult. Why does everything have to be so hard?*

"We might not have much of a history but we have the possibility of a wonderful future."

They reached his carriage and he helped her in. She sat across from him in the coach.

"We're going to a restaurant called Snyder's Clam Shack, down on the wharf. The establishment is an oyster saloon. I love oysters. Have you ever had oysters, m'dear?"

"I have. I don't like them." She found she was a bit apprehensive about a restaurant with the word 'shack' in the name, but if Harry thought the establishment was appropriate, so be it.

"You'll have to try them here. They are the best I've ever had...quite...tasty. They do, of course, have other offerings at the restaurant for your perusal."

"I should warn you now that I have a good appetite. I don't eat like a bird as some of the women of today are prone to do and I'm not ashamed."

"Good. I like a woman with a zest for life. That's one of the qualities that came across in your letters. Your love for life and for adventure." He reached across the carriage and took her hand in his. "We'll have a great adventure if you marry me, Cora."

She felt herself swaying in his favor at his words, but was adventure what she craved or just a home and children?

Harry let go of her hand and leaned back in his seat. He picked nonexistent lint from his sleeve. "There is one, tiny thing I didn't mention in our correspondence. I wanted you to meet her before you made any decisions."

"Her?" Cora raised an eyebrow and lowered her chin a notch. Here was the catch to the situation. "Meet her?"

"Yes. My mother lives with me and would live with us."

She blinked several times. She almost shouted. "You didn't think that was important enough to mention? That your mother would be living with us? When would you have told me if Asa hadn't shown up? Before or after the ceremony?"

"Now Cora, please it's not like that. She's a lovely woman. You'll like her, really you will."

"What if she doesn't like me? What then?" She remembered her friend, Maude. Her mother-in-law lived with her for several years before the old woman died. Maude said it was hell. Her husband never took her side in arguments and the old biddy had delighted in torturing Maude with her words. "As long as we're talking about things happening before we marry, you should know that I'm opening a dress shop and I intend to keep the business after I marry...*whoever* I marry. Do you have a problem with that?" She had to keep herself under control, otherwise she'd be yelling at him.

Of course, that probably wouldn't matter in the place he'd brought her for dinner. They arrived at a one-story wooden building that had seen better days. It was down by the wharf, clearly in a part of town no self-respecting lady would be seen in. There were sailors and dock workers coming in and out of the building, she noticed after a quick glance around. All the structures were shabby looking, some with shutters hanging off to one side of the windows. She heard tinny piano music coming from inside the building.

Snyder's Clam Shack was a boisterous place. But she saw she was the only woman who was having dinner and she was definitely overdressed for the occasion. The other women she saw were waiting tables and serving drinks. She was not impressed with Harry's choice of a restaurant.

She was also not ignorant of the reputation of oysters. Cora knew they were supposed to be an aphrodisiac and wondered at Harry's motives. Surely he wasn't attempting to seduce her on their first dinner engagement.

Given his choices and springing his mother on her, Cora had had enough for the evening.

"Harry, I want to go back to the hotel."

"Cora, if this is about my mother...we can talk—"

"It's about your decisions. Waiting to tell me about your mother and then bringing me here," she waved her arm to encompass the restaurant, "for our first dinner is beyond the pale. I said I have a zest for life, not that I wanted to eat dinner in a...a sailors saloon."

Harry looked around and then he grew red in the neck and ears.

"Cora, I'm so sorry. I wasn't thinking at all. I simply wanted to bring you to one of my favorite restaurants. I've never paid much attention to the clientele, just the oysters. Please forgive my *terrible* judgment. I haven't been here in sometime and I clearly wasn't thinking about the clientele, just about the food."

"I notice you don't apologize for waiting to tell me about your mother. That is the most important part of this entire debacle of an evening." She jumped to her feet. "Please take me back to the hotel."

"Of course, right away."

He followed her out of the saloon to his carriage and helped her in.

Once they were on their way, Harry sat next to her and tried to take her hand in his. She would have none of it, shook his hand off hers and moved to the seat across from him.

"Cora, please, give me another chance. Let me take you to a nice dinner in a fine restaurant as I should have to begin with."

She crossed her arms over her chest and looked at him in the seat across from her. Should she? Right now she was pretty disgusted, but she did have a signed contract with him and should probably give him the chance to make it right. After all, what Asa had done was more grievous, and she was giving him another chance.

"All right, Harry. We'll try again. Tomorrow I'm spending with Asa, but the day after that is yours."

"Thank you, Cora. You won't regret your decision, I promise."

"Harry, when were you going to tell me about your mother? Really?"

"To be honest, I was going to wait until

after we'd married. I didn't want you to leave me because of her."

She gasped. "Don't you think that is deceitful? What if she and I don't get along? Who are you going to choose then?"

"You'll get along. Everyone gets along with my mother."

"Why do I not believe you? If that was true, you would have told me in our correspondence or at the very least when we met—"

He blushed and Cora knew he was lying. His mother was definitely not someone people got along with.

Harry leaned forward, his eyebrows together in a frown. "Be reasonable, Cora. I didn't have a chance to tell you last night after Asa showed up and you wouldn't have come if you'd known about her before. Be honest."

Cora chewed her lower lip, "I suppose you're right. And for that reason, we are starting fresh, like tonight never happened. And remember, I do not like oysters. They are slimy and nasty."

Harry laughed. "Note taken. No oysters. If I desire them, I'll go to Snyder's Clam Shack by myself. Good enough?"

She smiled and nodded. "Good enough."

They'd settled the situation about the restaurant but not his mother. What could she do except meet her?

The carriage pulled up in front of the hotel.

Harry walked her to her room.

"Dare I hope for a kiss?"

"That's awfully forward, don't you think? Even if it wasn't, after this evening that would be asking too much indeed."

"Well, you can't blame a man for asking a beautiful woman for a kiss."

"I'm flattered you think me beautiful but you still get no kiss."

He chuckled, then raised her hand to his lips and gently kissed the top. "This will have to do then."

Cora opened the door to her room. "Goodnight, Harry. I'll see you day after tomorrow."

"I can barely wait until then." He gave her a bow of his head, turned and departed down the hall.

That night Cora wrote in her diary.

June 3, 1867
Dear Diary,

My first outing with Harry was a total disaster. He took me to a sailor's saloon for dinner, and then had the audacity to tell me his mother would be living with us. After that, the choice of restaurant was insignificant, though still a poor choice, and makes me wonder about Harry. Does he always make such poor decisions? Does he make better business decisions? He must or he wouldn't stay president of his bank.

He told me his mother and I would like each other. When I heard him add 'everyone does' my suspicious nature came to the fore. I wonder how many other people he's had to say that to. I have the feeling his mother is anything but likeable but I will try to keep an open mind.

CHAPTER 3

Twenty minutes later, Harry entered his home and gave his coat, hat, and gloves to Jenkins, his butler.

"Your mother awaits your return in the library, sir."

Harry sighed. He'd hoped to put off seeing his mother until tomorrow, but he supposed the interview couldn't be helped.

After entering the library, he headed straight to the sidebar and the carafe of good Irish whiskey he kept there. He poured two fingers into a glass.

His mother sat on the settee reading in front of the fire, in her midnight blue dressing gown.

"You're home early. I assume dinner didn't go very well." She didn't look up from her book.

"No, I made a grave error tonight. I took her to my favorite restaurant."

His mother dropped her book and sat upright on the sofa. "You took her to that oyster saloon? Are you mad? This was your first outing and you didn't think you needed to impress her by perhaps taking her to the Cliff House, for instance." She got up and strode over to him.

"Cora said she had a good appetite and I thought—"

"You didn't think." She slapped him upside his head. "You thought to save a few dollars by taking her to a cheap restaurant instead of a good one. Well, it would serve you right if she chooses the other man to marry. How could you do this to us?"

"I'm sorry, Mother. I'll take her to the Cliff House on my next occasion with her."

"You mean she has agreed to another dinner engagement? Did you tell her about me?"

He nodded. "I told her you live with me."

"Ha!" His mother laughed heartily. "What will she think when she finds out you live with me and it's my money you've been spending?"

"I have a good position at the bank." He squared his shoulders. "I'm president for goodness sakes."

"Yes." She pointed her finger at him. "You have a gambling problem, too. What would this pretty little woman think if she knew you spend all of your salary in the poker hells?"

Harry downed the drink in one gulp, and then poured himself another, three fingers this time. He walked to the fireplace, turned and faced his mother.

"She won't find out because no one will tell her. By the time she learns, it will be too late and hopefully she will be pregnant."

"You'd better hope so. The only reason I'm funding this venture is to get a grandchild. One that hopefully will turn out better than you did."

"I know I'm a great disappointment, Mother. You've told me enough times." He drank his whiskey and walked back to the bar for another.

"Go to bed, Harry. You've had enough to drink. Think about your evening and how the next one will be better. You can't make mistakes again or we'll lose her."

He set glass on the counter with a thud. "Yes, Mother. Goodnight."

"Goodnight."

Harry left the library and his bitch of a mother. If he didn't need her to pay his bills he'd leave. Ah, but there was the rub. He did need her and she needed him. Only he could give her the grandchild she desired. He wondered what would become of Cora after she'd given them the baby. Would his mother keep her around for another child, a spare? Or would she dispose of her as she had his other wives when they couldn't produce a child?

*****

The next day Cora knocked on Annie's door. It was six o'clock in the morning and she hoped it wasn't too rude to be here at this hour.

The entrance opened and her friend, Annie Markum, stood in her dressing gown, though mostly hidden by the wooden door.

Concern crossed Annie's lovely face. "Cora? What's the matter?"

Cora felt awful for causing her friend any alarm but she needed to talk to someone. "Annie, can I come in?"

"Of course." She stepped to the side and

Cora entered the room, which was just like Cora's. Done in shades of blue with wooden floors and dark blue rugs under the table and by the bed, the room was inviting.

"Let's sit. I don't have coffee or tea but we can have water."

"No, nothing, thanks."

Wide-eyed, Annie asked, as they walked to the table. "What did you think of Nellie's quick wedding yesterday?"

"The ceremony was nice." Cora sat in one of the two wooden chairs at the small table. "Even if the decision to wed happened so fast."

Nellie Wallace decided to marry Blake Malone the day after they met. They both thought waiting, when they had already determined they would definitely marry, was ridiculous and so they'd done the deed. Blake had the license all ready to go, and the judge, a friend of Blake's, had been happy to perform the ceremony.

"I wish I felt as strongly about William as Nellie did about Blake," said Annie, a wistful note in her voice. "I think with her it was love at first sight, like she was hit with a lightning bolt. Though I remember she looked at Blake's picture all the time while we were on board the ship."

"I think the situation was the same with him, but they still have to get to know each other," said Cora. "What's wrong with William? He seemed like a nice enough man when we met down in the lobby."

"Oh, he is," said Annie quickly. "He's very nice but driven and he's so much older than me. I hadn't realized what a difference our ages would make. All he could talk about is his work. He's an importer and brings in things like silk, coffee, tea and spices to be sold here in San Francisco and shipped to other cities up and down the coast. When the railroad is completed, he'll start shipping them to the rest of the country. He figures to make a fortune."

"So, you'll be marrying a rich man. That's not so bad, is it?"

"No," she sighed deeply. "I just wonder if I'm the wife he needs. I'm a poor preacher's daughter, what do I know about being a hostess and that kind of thing. But never mind about me. What brings you to my door so early in the morning?"

"Harry and Asa. The dinner with Harry was a disaster. He took me to his favorite restaurant which was a place called Snyder's

Clam Shack. I suppose the choice would have been fine if he knew I liked oysters or clams, but I don't. First, he should have asked me if I liked that particular food and second, I expected something a little grander. I mean even the restaurant at this hotel is nicer. The place he took me is for sailors or dockworkers not gentlemen on an outing with a lady."

"Well, maybe he just wanted you to know what he likes," said Annie.

She knew her friend was trying to be helpful, but Cora still felt humiliated.

"I feel like Harry didn't care enough to think about what I might like. If he acts like that now, what about after we marry, if we do? Will I be even less important then, because he, 'has' me and there's nothing I can do?"

"Let me get dressed and we'll go to the restaurant in the lobby and talk more. I can't imagine what he was thinking, but I doubt he meant to insult you."

Annie donned a beautiful blue walking dress Cora had made for her on the voyage.

Cora wore a vibrant yellow day dress, and knew they both looked good as they went downstairs to breakfast.

The tables were as welcoming in the light of day as they had the night she had dinner with Asa. They were settled at one, and the waiter came by and took their order.

"So," said Annie, "what is the matter? That Harry took you to a poor choice of restaurant?"

"That's part of it." Cora rearranged the silverware around her plate, and then did it again.

Annie reached over and stilled her hands. "Stop. Just tell me what concerns you."

Cora nodded. "The other part is he didn't tell me his mother would be living with us when we got married. I'm not sure I can handle taking care of both Harry and his mother. What about my business? What about any children we might have?"

"Seems to me that you're worrying for nothing. It's not unusual for parents to live with their children when they get older. You know that."

"Yes. I know. I'm concerned over the fact he didn't tell me before. I feel like there are other things he might be hiding, if he hid this. This is important. I should have had a choice."

Annie laughed. "Then it's a good thing Asa showed up. You do have a choice now. I think you're just nervous about making it."

The waiter came back with their breakfast orders.

Cora loved breakfast. It was her favorite meal of the day. Today, she'd ordered two fried eggs, a slice of ham, a rasher of bacon, fried potatoes, and toasted sourdough bread, along with coffee and a glass of milk.

She took a sip of her coffee and then salted and peppered her eggs. Taking her knife and fork she slashed back and forth, cutting up the eggs and spreading the yolk over all the white.

"If you wanted scrambled eggs, why didn't you order them," said Annie with a smile after watching Cora.

"I didn't want scrambled eggs." She used her fork to point. "I like the runny yolk, but I don't like the white, so I spread the yolk over the white and then it's all good."

Annie shook her head and took a spoonful of the oatmeal she'd ordered with toast and coffee.

They were quiet for a few moments while they both ate and stopped their bellies from growling with hunger.

"Now," said Annie. "I feel much better. So, you're concerned Harry is hiding something. What?"

Cora rolled her eyes. "If I knew what, I wouldn't be worried about it."

"Good point."

"I don't know what to do." Cora signaled for the server and more coffee.

"I think you go on with your plan. You let both men court you, you meet the mother, and you open your dress shop. Then if you decide not to marry either man, you'll still have your shop."

"You know, when I came out here, I was fully convinced I would marry Harry and we'd live happily ever after, like in a fairy tale." She slumped in her chair. "Now I'm discovering there is more to the fairy tale than just the happy ending."

"Of course, there is. I think, too, that you must still have feelings for Asa, or you wouldn't have considered his suit after all this time."

Cora felt the warmth rise up her neck to her cheeks.

"See, you're blushing. I'm right," said Annie pointing at Cora.

"Fine. I admit I do. When I first received

his proposal, I didn't even hesitate. I wanted to marry him and I wish now that we had before he left for war. But he wanted to wait. He didn't want to make me a widow if he got killed."

Cora ate more of her breakfast, but now the food did not satisfy the need inside her and she shoved away her plate.

Annie raised her eyebrows. "You really are upset if you're not eating breakfast."

"I am. I want to give both Harry and Asa the benefit of the doubt but right now, I'm not feeling very generous toward either of them. Although, Asa did take me to a nice dinner and we had a wonderful time."

Annie reached across the table and put her hand atop Cora's. "See, that was good. As to the rest, you're just scared. It's a big step, getting married. I know. I'm feeling scared myself, but this is what I signed up for. William and I are going to take a little time, but we will marry by the end of the month, if not sooner."

"That's just a few weeks away."

"It's enough. If I had my way, I'd do what Nellie did and marry right away. No one really knows anyone until after you're married anyway, whether you've been courting or not. The best most marriages can hope for is friendship."

"That's ridiculous. I fully expect to love my husband. If not right away, at some point down the road."

"Father says that earthly love is not real. Only Godly love is real."

Shaking her head, Cora rolled her eyes. "Your father is a preacher. What do you expect him to say?"

"Well, I…"

"Never mind. Thanks for letting me talk to you. I think I'll take your advice and just let them court me. The truth will out during that process, I believe."

Annie folded her napkin and placed it neatly on top of her toast plate. "Good. Now let's go back upstairs and you can help me with my mother's wedding dress. It's a beautiful peach colored satin but I need the garment altered, and since you're a seamstress, I thought…"

"Of course," Cora smiled. "I'd love to help. With your coloring, the gown should look beautiful on you."

"I look like my mother. Sometimes I think that's why my father didn't have much time for me. I reminded him of her and he missed her too much. At least that's what I tell myself."

Cora took Annie's arm and they walked across the lobby together before starting up the staircase.

Feeling more lighthearted since talking to Annie, she said, "You're father was wrong to ignore you. Let's go see about that dress."

CHAPTER 4

Asa picked up a picnic basket from the hotel kitchen. They'd been very helpful in providing not only the basket of food but a place to take Cora as well. He waited for her in the lobby, as she requested. He knew she didn't want him to have to walk up and down all those stairs but he didn't mind. His prosthetic leg was just another part of him now and he was no longer ashamed. Dr. Reynolds had helped him see that he was still the same inside even though he now had a limp.

Cora glided down the staircase toward him, a vision in lavender. She wore her hair up and a wide-brimmed hat that matched the dress was tied under her chin.

She waved. "Asa."

"Cora," he called and waved back.

When she got to him, he gave her a kiss on the cheek, just as he used to before he left for the war.

"You look lovely," he said.

She ducked her head and blushed prettily. "Thank you. You look awfully handsome yourself today."

"And I look horrible on other days?" he teased.

"No, that's not what I meant," she sputtered.

He laughed. "I'm just teasing you."

"Oh you, rascal." She laughed with him.

He held out his arm for her and she put hers through the crook in his elbow.

"One of the hotel waiters gave me the directions to a place for our picnic where we can overlook not only the ocean, but the city, too. Are you ready?"

"Actually, I'd like to stop by my friend Nellie's house. I want you to meet her."

"Didn't she and her husband just get married?" He frowned. "Won't they be on a honeymoon now?"

"No, Nellie has two children and she and Blake are still getting to know one another."

He nodded. "Well, I've rented the

carriage and driver for the day, so we can go wherever you want."

She grinned. "Wonderful. I know you'll like Nellie."

"What about Blake?"

"I don't know him, myself, so I can't say."

From the hotel, the streets wound around buildings, some old, some not, before heading up the hill to the Malone's. The city was a font of hills with roads leading up them to homes and down into town which was flat. New structures were being built every day. San Francisco was still booming. The downtown area was already cramped with structures and was continuing to expand. Cora hoped to make sense of it all, while opening her shop.

Arriving at Nellie and Blake's, Asa helped Cora out of the coach. Together they walked up the stairs to the front door where Asa raised the knocker, shaped like a lion's head and let the tongue of the lion drop twice. The door opened quickly and a man in a black suit with a crisp white shirt and tie greeted them.

"Sir, madam, how may I be of service?"

"We're here to see Mrs. Nellie Malone,"

said Cora. "Please tell her that her friend Cora is here to see her."

"Yes, madam. Please come in and wait in the foyer."

He held open the door for them to enter and then turned and walked down the richly carpeted hallway toward the back of the house.

The foyer where they stood was two stories tall, with marble tile on the floor and intricately carved wainscoting. There was a grand, curved staircase to the right of the carpeted hall way. At the top Asa could see a hall leading off to the right and a curved walkway to the left leading to another hallway.

"It's quite lavish," observed Asa.

Cora laid her hand on his arm. "Blake is a very wealthy man. Don't feel like you have to compete with him."

"If this is what you want, I'll see you get it. I'm not without funds myself." Asa grinned. When he'd known her before, his aunt hadn't died leaving him as her only beneficiary. As a consequence, he was now a very wealthy man.

A lovely blond woman, in a dark blue dress hurried toward them.

"Cora. I hadn't expected to see you so soon," said the woman, taking both of Cora's hands, and bending to kiss her cheek.

"I hope we're not interrupting, dropping in unannounced."

"Not at all. You are always welcome. Let's go to the parlor. I've already sent James to find Blake."

They followed her down the hall to the second door on the right. A grand oak door opened into a large, inviting room. A green brocade settee and four, large, overstuffed chairs sat in front of the fire place. Two chairs on either end of the sofa, curved inward so the furniture formed a semi-circle in front of the hearth

"This is lovely," commented Cora.

"The room is beautiful. The whole house is actually. Blake has very good taste," agreed Nellie.

"Of course, I have good taste. I married you didn't I?"

A handsome man with dark brown hair came forward to Asa, hand outstretched.

"Blake Malone."

"Asa Woods and you already know Cora."

"Yes," said Blake, taking Cora's hand

and kissing it. "How nice to see you again. To what do we owe the pleasure?"

"Sit, sit, I'll ring for some refreshments. Wait a minute," Nellie stopped and, eyebrows lifted, turned toward Asa. "Aren't you supposed to be dead?" She stared while pulling the bell cord.

He sighed, fresh shame washed through him. "Yes, ma'am. It's a long story and I'd really prefer not to go into the details right now. Suffice it to say that my leg, and my fears, kept me from coming home to Cora."

The butler entered. "You rang, madam."

"Yes, please bring us some tea and cookies."

"Yes, madam." He bowed and left the room.

Cora sat on the settee and patted the seat beside her for Asa. "We stopped by because I wanted you to meet Asa, and to ask Blake if he knew a good location for a dress shop. I want to open one and I don't know the city, so I need some help."

Blake moved two of the chairs so they were across the coffee table from the settee. He helped Nellie into one and sat in the other. "Downtown would be best, but a location down there can be expensive. Let me see if I can find you a nice little storefront, perhaps just off Main Street. That would be cheaper and still close enough to get foot traffic as people shop."

"Oh, thank you. I knew you'd be able to help me. You don't know how much I appreciate it." Cora extended her hand over the table, Blake took it and they shook hands.

"Well that's taken care of, now where are you off to?" asked Nellie.

"A picnic," replied Cora.

The butler came back pushing a tea trolley. He set the service on the table in front of Nellie and then retreated with the cart.

She poured them each a cup of tea.

"Would you like milk or sugar?"

"No," said Asa and Cora together.

"A picnic? Oh, how lovely." Nellie looked at Blake, "We should do that? It would be a good way to see some of the city and we could take the children for them to play outside."

"Whatever you'd like m'dear," Blake took Nellie's hand and kissed it. "As soon as I can arrange it, but business must come first."

Nellie blushed a little, "Of course, Forgive me, I didn't mean to get in the way of business."

Even Asa could feel the tension in the air. "You know that Cora has two gentlemen courting her?"

Nellie's head snapped back to his and then to Cora. "Why, no I didn't know that, exactly. Though I wondered what happened to Harry Belcher. You talked about him on the voyage here."

"It's nothing really," said Cora with a shake of her head.

"*It* most certainly is something," said Asa. "Otherwise you'd just marry me and be done."

Cora narrowed her eyes and they flashed with anger. "You let me think you were dead for nearly two years. What I should do is marry Harry and be done with it."

"Now Cora," soothed Asa, "forget I mentioned it. Let's just go on our picnic and enjoy ourselves."

She took a deep breath. "You're right. Let's have some fun today."

That was one thing he'd always liked about Cora, she didn't stay mad for long.

"With other things on my mind, I forgot

to ask." Blake set down his cup and saucer on the table and took a small note book out of his pocket. "How big you want this space to be?"

Cora thought for a moment. "Well, you've been into a dress shop, have you not?"

He nodded. "Yes, of course."

"Well, I need one with a good-size front area where the mirrors will be, and of course, room for a couple of comfortable chairs for the husbands who accompany my customers. But the back where the actual work takes place would need to be about twice as big as the showroom since there will just be me working there, at least for the time being. I know that's not very helpful. You probably want measurements, don't you? Well, I want the front to be about ten feet by twelve feet. The back room needs to be at least ten by twenty-four feet but twenty by thirty would be better. I want to call the business Cora's Creations or Creations by Cora. What do you think?"

"You've been thinking about this for a long time." Asa was proud Cora had taken the time to know what she wanted.

"I have. Since before I became a mail-order bride. I just didn't have the money when I was in New York."

"I love the names. Either one would be good. I prefer Creations by Cora. It sounds more 'upscale'," said Nellie. "I'll be your first customer and Annie will be your second. Did you decide about making children's clothes?"

"Only for you. I want to concentrate on ladies' gowns and undergarments."

"Well don't worry about the children then. I'm sure there are plenty of places to get their clothes." She looked pointedly at her husband. "Blake will take me."

"I'm taking Henry to my tailor." Blake hedged a bit by sipping at his tea. "I admit I have no idea where to take you for Violet's clothing."

"Well then," said Cora. "I'll make Violet's dresses. She can have ones that match her mother's. There's always enough material left for a little girls dress, when she's as small as Violet, anyway."

The door to the library burst open and the subject of the conversation came flying through.

"Cora!" Violet yelled as soon as she saw her and made a beeline for the settee.

Cora was used to this, and caught Violet when she launched herself at her. "Hello, my little love. How are you?"

Violet hugged her tight around the neck, and then sat in Cora's lap. "I'm good. Me and Bertha sleep in a really big room with lots of toys. Mama calls it a mersry."

"Nursery, love," corrected Cora.

"Right, dats what I said. Anyway and Henry gots a room on the third floor. I looked down from his window and it's way high up."

"You be careful when you're up in his room. You should probably play on the floor, not on the window seat," said Nellie, a hand at her throat. She seemed alarmed at the idea of her daughter playing up so high.

"I'm sure she's been very careful, haven't you, Violet?" said Cora as she smoothed a circle on the little girl's back.

She nodded, her blond curls bouncing merrily.

"Yup. Henry make me get out so he could watch the boats."

Cora settled Violet on her lap, where she was happy to sit and chatter to everyone.

"Thank you, Blake, for doing this. I'm still at the hotel, so you can contact me there when you have a place for me to see. Are you sure it's not a imposition?"

"It's no problem at all. Any friend of Nellie's is a friend of mine, and I don't mind helping out."

"Violet, honey, why don't you go find Henry and play with him for a while?" said Nellie. "Cora and her friend have to leave pretty soon and Mama and Blake want to talk to them."

"Okay. I love you, Cora." Violet gave her a big hug and kissed her cheek.

"I love you, too, sweet cheeks."

Violet jumped down and ran from the room.

"Does she ever walk anywhere?" asked Asa, as he watched the little girl leave.

"Never," said her mother. "And when she sees Blake she usually runs and jumps on him. She's taken a definite liking to her new father."

"She and I have a special relationship." Blake nodded and laughed. "We loved each other from the first moment. I can't tell you why, we just did."

"Well, I think it's wonderful," said Cora. "But we do have to leave. Asa has the carriage and driver for the day, but I don't want to leave him out there too long, that would be rude."

"We can ask him to come in, if you like," said Nellie.

"No, that's all right, we should get going so we can have our picnic. The place the hotel recommended is more than an hour away, they said. It's on a hill overlooking the bay and the city. They said it's by a lovely restaurant called the Cliff House."

"I know the location they're talking about," Blake nodded. "And the ride will be a good hour from here. But the place is lovely and you should enjoy yourselves."

Everyone stood. Cora and Nellie locked arms and walked through the library door.

"I'm so glad you stopped by," said Nellie when they got to the foyer. "We simply must stay in touch with each other."

"Of course." Cora turned to Blake with a smile. "I look forward to hearing from you. I can't wait to start my business. I brought three trunks of sewing supplies and material. While I wait, I'll start making a couple of sample dresses, and I'll be ready to go by the time you find me something."

Blake took her hand and kissed it. "I'll do my very best for you. I should be able to let you know in a few days." Then he turned to Asa. "You have your work cut out for you. These ladies are quite independent, if my wife is any indication."

"Now, Blake," said Nellie with a smile.

"Oh, I already knew that," said Asa. "Cora was always an independent sort, even when she was a child."

"And I intend to stay that way," said Cora. "Are you sure you want to marry me?"

"Absolutely," nodded Asa, then he turned to Blake and Nellie. "Thank you for letting us visit and Blake let me add my thanks to Cora's. I've never seen her so excited as she is about this shop."

"Anytime. Glad to help."

When Cora and Asa got to the carriage, they turned and waved at Nellie and Blake who stood in their doorway.

"They seem like a nice couple," said Asa, who sat next to Cora in the carriage.

"Yes, they do and they are. I'm so glad Blake is willing to help me. I had intended ask Harry, but I just didn't feel right about it. Thank you for letting us stop by here today."

Asa took Cora's hand. "I'll do anything

you want me to. Just ask and it's yours."

"Oh, Asa." She put her hand over the top of his. "Do you remember the fun we used to have—you, Virgil and I? You two used to let me come along when you went fishing in the summer and skating in the winter. I know I was just a kid, but you both made me feel welcome. That's a big thing for a little girl."

"I remember lots of things. More than you can imagine."

"That's nice of you to say, but why would you remember stuff like that? I was just a kid who was probably a pest to you most of the time. You and Virgil were...are eight years older than me. That was a lot then, though it doesn't seem like so much now."

"Not true. You were a sweet little girl, who grew into a beautiful woman."

"Ah, Asa." She ducked and then laid her head upon his shoulder. "You say the nicest things."

"I only speak the truth, you know me."

They rode like that for a long way— neither of them speaking, just reveling in each other's company. The carriage finally stopped and the driver, a big burley man with black hair and kind eyes, opened the door.

"Here ya, go, mate and miss. I come here sometime with the missus and youngun's. There's a nice little patch of green and some trees just over that little rise. I'll be right here when yer ready to go."

"Thank you, sir," said Cora.

"I ain't no sir, I'm just Jeb," replied the driver.

"Well, thank you, Jeb. We didn't introduce ourselves before. I'm Cora." She held out her hand.

"Pleased to make your acquaintance, Miss Cora." He took off his glove and wiped his hand on his coat before shaking hers.

"And I'm Asa," he shook Jeb's hand as well. "We'll be back after a bit."

"No, hurry. I got a book and my lunch here, I'll be fine."

Asa took Cora's hand and they walked over the small rise. When they reached the top, they looked down on a small patch of green grass at the base of two trees. The spot was sitting right along the edge of the cliff. From there they could see the city and the bay and watch the ships coming and going.

He set down the picnic basket and

opened it. Inside was a blanket, which he spread on the grass. Underneath was a bottle of wine, two glasses and a corkscrew, roast beef sandwiches, a container of potato salad, cheese, grapes, apples and both sugar and oatmeal cookies.

"Oh, my, this looks wonderful. Thank you, Asa." She tucked her legs underneath her and sat on the blanket. "I haven't been on a picnic since..." she paused. "Well, since the one where you asked me to marry you."

Asa laughed. "That's the last time I was on one, too." He eased himself down to his knees and then sat next to her on the blanket.

"The scenery is lovely," she said.

"I agree. I've never seen anything lovelier."

She looked up and saw him looking at her, not at the ocean. She ducked her head again and felt her cheeks heat.

"Would you like a glass of wine?" he asked.

"I'd love one."

He took the corkscrew and opened the wine, poured them each a glass of the dark red liquid and then held up his. "To us. May we always find joy in the simple things and in each other."

Cora wasn't sure she should toast to them as a couple, so she said, "To friends. May we always be so."

Asa smiled and clinked their glasses. "To friends."

She let go of the breath she'd been holding, relieved that he hadn't gotten upset with her not agreeing with his toast. She wondered if Harry would be as easy-going.

There was still something about Harry that concerned her but she couldn't put her finger on what her actual concerns were. More than just a poor choice of restaurant, she was sure he was hiding something. Maybe just the news about his mother, but Cora thought there was more. In any case, she wouldn't think about that now.

Now was for Asa and this wonderful picnic.

CHAPTER 5

Harry picked up Cora the following Sunday to meet his mother. Cora dressed with special care. She wore a burgundy dress with matching hat and black gloves. She thought she looked spectacular, the color of the garment making her pale skin glow.

After deciding she didn't want him coming to her room, she walked across the lobby to meet Harry. He wasn't paying attention but was reading a newspaper. When Cora walked up to him he quickly put down the paper but she saw he'd been looking at the horse racing results.

"Cora. You look lovely m'dear." He took her hand and kissed the top as he usually did.

"Thank you, Harry."

She thought he looked a little tired, like he hadn't been sleeping well or had perhaps been sleeping in a chair. His hair was a bit mussed and his suit not as sharply pressed as she'd seen the garment before.

"Shall we go? Mother is anxious to meet you."

Cora swallowed hard. "As I am to meet her." The lie came easier than she thought it would. She wasn't looking forward to meeting Mrs. Belcher at all. She'd never been good with her own parents much less someone else's.

After a short carriage ride, they pulled onto a circular driveway and up in front of a lovely three-story mansion. Harry had said he was rich, but she hadn't known how rich until now.

The house was a gorgeous red-brick home with matching sharply pointed roofs on either end and a flat roof with four dormer windows in the middle. On the ground floor was a circular window seat in what she assumed was the parlor to the left of the entrance. The massive wooden entrance door had a white arch above, and a knocker the shape of a eagle's head.

Harry hopped out of the carriage and turned to help Cora.

They stood in the driveway and looked up at the house.

"Wh…what do you think?"

"It's quite spectacular. I never imagined you lived in such a magnificent home."

She watched him relax and smile.

"Thank you. That means a lot coming from you."

She was surprised that he would want her opinion, but it pleased her nonetheless.

"I don't know why you should care what I think, but thank you."

"I care because I want you to like the home you will live in."

She turned to him and frowned. "Assuming I choose you to marry."

"I have no doubt you will."

She cocked her eyebrow. "Awfully sure of yourself, aren't you?"

Rocking back on his heels, he grabbed his coat by the lapels and puffed out his chest. "Yes, I am," he smiled showing straight white teeth.

Cora wanted to wipe the grin off his face. She wasn't sure who, if anyone, she would choose, but the more he spoke the more she pulled away. No one would tell her what to do and who to like or who to choose. Not Asa. Not Harry and most assuredly not Harry's mother.

A butler in a black suit, white shirt and tie opened the door before they had the chance.

"Thank you, Jenkins. Please tell my mother we are here and to meet us in the library."

"Yes, sir, I would, but madam already awaits you in the parlor and requests your presence there upon your arrival."

"All right, parlor it is." He held out his arm to her. "M'dear."

Cora put her hand through the crook of his elbow and together, they walked into the parlor which was the room next to the entrance. Entering the room she saw she was right about the circular window seat.

Mrs. Belcher sat upon it waiting for them.

The seat appeared to be well cushioned with matching flowered curtains hanging over the windows. The rest of the room was completed in various shades of green. The wall paper was dark green stripes alternating with white ones. The drapes over the windows, except the window seat were solid forest green and tied back with black satin ties.

"Harry, darling. Is this the sweet girl you're planning on marrying?"

His mother's voice was sugary sweet and grated on Cora's nerves. But she pasted on a smile.

"Yes, Mother. May I introduce Miss Cora Jones? Cora, my mother Henrietta Belcher."

"How do you do, Mrs. Belcher?" Cora moved forward to take the woman's outstretched hand.

"I'm lovely, my girl, but you must call me Henrietta, at least until I can convince you to call me Mother."

Cora raised her eyebrows. Her impression of this woman was not getting better. Not only was her voice awful, but she practically had Cora already married to Harry. Huh! Mother, indeed.

Henrietta stood and walked to the green paisley upholstered settee in front of the fireplace. "Please, sit, Cora." She patted the seat next to her.

Harry sat in one of the Queen Anne chairs across from them.

"So tell me about yourself. I understand you are a seamstress."

With Henrietta's condescending tone, she might as well have called Cora a char woman. "Yes. I'm planning on opening my own dress shop with my original designs called Creations by Cora. I'll also make whatever dresses the client likes from other designers, of course."

"I would think so. You're not well-known enough to have clientele for your own designs yet." She quickly added. "But I'm sure you will. I understand you plan on working after you marry. What about after you have children? I assume you would remain home then?"

"Yes, ma'am. More than likely, though I will hopefully have seamstresses working for me by that time and will simply do the designing."

Henrietta frowned momentarily but recovered and flashed a smile. "I see. Well, you and Harry will have to discuss that when the time comes."

Cora had enough. "*Mrs. Belcher.* I don't know what Harry has told you, but I have another suitor and have *not* made up my mind about who I should marry. Or *if* I will marry either man."

Henrietta gave a shake of her head. "Oh, Harry has told me all of that, my dear, but I have faith in my son. He will win your heart."

You have more faith than I do.

"Now, Mother. You're going to chase Cora away with all this talk of marriage. Nothing has been decided."

Well, at least Harry seemed to understand the situation. He wasn't forcing her into a decision, which was a good thing for him, because he would lose.

"You're absolutely right, son. Forgive me, Cora." She reached over and patted Cora's lap. "I am simply anxious for my son to be happily settled down, that's all. You can't blame an old woman for that, now can you?"

Cora cocked an eyebrow and answered cautiously. "No, ma'am, I don't suppose I can. Everyone wants their children to be happy."

The butler entered.

"Dinner is served, madam."

"Ah, very good, Jenkins. Harry you will escort me to the dining room. Cora will follow."

They walked down the hall past several closed doors to the last room on the right. The room was done in shades of blue from the striped wall paper to the Persian rugs on the floor. The dining hall actually was quite lovely and Cora felt more comfortable here. The room seemed to soothe her.

The large, dark wood table was polished to a high sheen and had candelabras at either end. Formal place settings were situated at one end.

Harry helped his mother to the chair at the end of the table. Then he helped Cora into hers on his mother's left before taking his seat on Henrietta's right.

"Wine, please, Jenkins," said Henrietta.

The butler brought a bottle to the table and poured a small amount of the blood red liquid into Harry's glass. He swished the wine around, stuck his nose in the glass and sniffed.

"Very good, Jenkins."

The butler curtly nodded his head and poured a measured amount in all of their glasses.

Henrietta raised her glass. "To my new daughter-in-law."

Cora's whole body stiffened and she set

down her glass. "I'm *not* your new daughter-in-law and at this rate I will never be. You're words, gestures and the pressure you're putting on me is exceedingly rude." Cora was panting by the end of her tirade, but she felt much better. "I find I no longer have an appetite. I think it would be best if Harry took me back to my hotel."

"I'm very sorry, Cora," Henrietta sputtered, her wide-eyed gaze moving between the other two. "I have been boorish in my attitude toward you. Of course, you and Harry need to take this at your own pace. Forgive me."

Cora knew she was being rude right back. But for a moment she actually thought about telling the old woman that she could keep her son, but she did like Harry and now understood where his attitude came from. His mother was obviously pushing him and he was responding in the only way he could to get the woman off his back.

"Yes, ma'am, but I would still like to go back to my hotel. I have a headache and fear I would not be good company this evening."

"Of course." She raised her arm and snapped her fingers. "Jenkins, have the carriage brought around."

"Yes, madam," He left the room.

"Stay Cora. She'll behave," promised Harry.

"Not this evening. Perhaps another."

"Harry, leave the poor girl alone. There, now you'll be able to return, but the carriage won't be up for a few minutes, let's go ahead and have a glass of wine."

"No, thank you." Cora put her hand over her glass as Harry started to pour her more of the red liquid. "I actually am not much of a drinker. I prefer tea or coffee. Mostly tea."

She saw a flash of anger in Henrietta's eyes before the woman murmured, "Of course, you would. Next time I'll be sure and have a pot of tea, just for you."

Cora stood. "Harry, shall we?" She turned her gaze on Henrietta. "Until next time, madam."

Henrietta stood as well. "Yes, my dear. Until next time and I promise to be on my best behavior."

Cora nodded and walked out of the room with Harry following her.

*****

After dropping Cora off, Harry returned home and found his mother in the library.

"What did you think you were doing?"

He walked to the side bar and poured himself a whiskey. *Three fingers should do it, at least to start.* "Do you think you can bully her like you did those other women? Cora is different. When will you get that through your head?"

"I'm sorry, Harry I wasn't thinking. I assumed she'd be as malleable as your other wives were. Most women of her age are still easily led. I was wrong." She waved her hand. "But no matter, we'll get her to marry us...you. We will get a grandchild."

Harry downed the amber liquid. "I don't know why having a grandchild is so important right now. I don't plan on dying anytime soon."

"But I am dying soon. The doctors don't give me much hope and I need to know that our family lives on. I intend to make the child my heir so you don't spend all of your inheritance at the racetrack or gaming tables."

"Aren't you afraid I might kill you before you change your will?"

"I've already changed it. The only guarantee you have of any income is to get me a child. If there is no child by the time I die, all of my money goes to charity." She raised an eyebrow. "My efforts to get into Heaven."

Harry seriously had considered murdering her to get out from under her thumb, but she outmaneuvered him yet again. He laughed joylessly. "Into Heaven after what you've done? I don't think murderers are allowed, no matter how much they pay to get in."

"Perhaps, but if I go to Hell, at least I'm comforted knowing you'll be along later. I definitely won't be alone there."

*****

Five days later, Cora grinned at Blake who sat across from her in his carriage. "I'm so excited and amazed that you could find an empty space so quickly."

"I happened to know the space would be coming available. My tailor needed a larger shop and found one, so his old location is up for lease. The rent for the building is a very good value at seventy-five dollars per month. I know it sounds like a lot, but wait until you see it."

They pulled up in front of a building on Howard Street, half a block off Main Street in downtown San Francisco. There were two display windows, one on either side of the wooden door with a small window in the upper half.

"I've got the key, you want to go in?"

Cora held her hands together to keep from clapping with excitement. "Oh, yes, please."

Blake unlocked the door and held it open. She went through, her heart pounding in her chest so hard she was sure Blake could hear it.

The front part of the space was set up for showing the clothes to husbands or paramours and for seeing the creations on the client. Mirrors were set up in two corners and along the back wall, so the client could see herself at any angle. And it was furnished with comfortable-looking chairs for the gentlemen to wait.

Through a door in the middle of the back wall was the work area. A small area was set up for taking measurements. Behind that was a large flat table for cutting patterns and enough room for four seamstresses to work, two on each side.

The rooms were much larger than Cora had envisioned but the rent was very competitive and the space would require little changes to accommodate her needs.

"I'll take it." She turned in a circle, arms out, laughing. "It's perfect." She walked to Blake and kissed him on the cheek. "Thank you so much. I don't know what I would do without you and Nellie."

He cleared his throat in response to her praise.

"I'm glad I could be of help. I was fairly sure you would be taking the space and have the leasing agreement with me, if you'd like to look it over. All you have to do is sign it, if the terms are to your liking."

He handed Cora the rental papers.

She read them over quickly. "The terms are very generous. Why is that?"

"The owner is a friend of mine and he won't have it vacant at all which was worth it for him. The rent is the same he was charging Godfrey, my tailor."

"I'll sign it as soon as we get back to your house. Then I'll have to find a place to live."

"I saved the best for last. The living area."

Eyes wide at this unexpected news she questioned. "The living area?"

"Come with me." He took her through the sewing room to the back where there were two doors. One led outside to the alleyway, the other led to a set of stairs. They climbed them to a landing where there was another door. Blake entered first and held the door for Cora.

"It's not very big, but should suffice for a single lady. It's also fully furnished, which I thought you'd appreciate."

Cora looked around. They were standing in a living area, which included a settee in a solid shade of moss green with two overstuffed chairs upholstered with greenery and flowers of various colors.

The kitchen included a small two-burner stove, icebox and a sink with a pump. There was also a beautiful round oak table and four chairs with spoked backs.

Blake pointed at the counter. "There is water at the sink but you have to use the outhouse in the back in the courtyard."

"No problem. I can get used to that. I'm just happy there is water and I don't have to haul it up here."

On the other side of the living room was a door. She walked over, opened it and found herself looking at a bedroom containing a double bed, twin nightstands, a wardrobe, bureau and commode.

It's smaller than the house I had in New York and there are no servants, but I like it.

"It's lovely, Blake. I don't know what to say."

"Well, you can say, yes, and sign that lease. I was sure you would like it and had the agent take it off the market."

"I'd like to thank the landlord myself. Who is he?"

"Well…" He cleared his throat. "I own the building. I didn't want to say anything when you first broached the subject, in case my agent had rented it already, but he hadn't so here you are. I'm glad you like it."

"Like it. I love it. Thank you."

Blake took her back to his house where Nellie met them in the library. When they entered she hurried to Cora and brought her back to the settee. "Well, what did you think of it?" She seemed as excited as Cora was.

"It's wonderful. Did you know about it?"

Nellie shook her head. "Not until this morning when Blake told me. I'm so happy for you. Sit. Sit. Have some tea." Nellie lifted the pot and tilted it over a cup.

"No thank you. I'm too excited. I don't know how to thank you. When I get settled, you, Blake and the kids will have to come over for dinner. I'm a pretty good cook, if I do say so myself. We'll have to eat downstairs at the cutting table, but that will make it even more of an adventure for the children."

"We'd love to," said Blake. "Will Asa be there?"

"I don't know." Cora frowned. "I'm so conflicted between Harry and Asa. On the one hand, I contracted with Harry and came out here to marry him. On the other I had already agreed to marry Asa whom I've known all my life. And I admit I've always cared for Asa, even had a crush on him."

"And what about Harry? How do you feel about him?" asked Blake.

"He's nice enough. Although he makes poor choices and I think his mother is the one who runs his life." Cora twisted the handkerchief in her lap. "I don't know that I want an overbearing mother-in-law. Asa's parents are both dead, so that wouldn't be a problem."

"How is Harry's mother overbearing?" asked Nellie.

Cora let out a sigh. "She insists I'm marrying Harry and she won't take no for an answer. I'm almost afraid to turn down his proposal."

"I can do some checking into Harry's and his mother's background if you like," offered Blake from his seat in one of the leather chairs across from the settee where Nellie and Cora sat.

"Could you?" Cora was so relieved. "I normally wouldn't ask but there is just something wrong with Harry's relationship with his mother. I just can't put my finger on it."

CHAPTER 6

Two days after she'd signed the rental agreement with Blake, Cora asked Harry and Asa to help her move her trunks to her new home. Both men were more than willing to help, even if it meant being with each other rather than alone with her.

There were only five trunks. Three of them stayed downstairs in the cutting room because they were full of bolts of material, thread, notions, buttons and the like. She would have to buy a sewing machine and sew up a couple of samples. Cora brought pattern books with her from New York, and now that she had an address to send them to, 115 Howard Street, San Francisco, California, she would write for a subscription. She said the address over and over in her mind, relishing the fact that she had a home and a business. Her dreams were coming true.

She'd decided the name of her business would be Creations by Cora. She agreed with Nellie that Cora's Creations didn't have the upper crust sound she needed to attract the elite of San Francisco society. She would need to work hard to make those contacts. Perhaps Blake had associates whose wives would be willing to try a new seamstress. In any case she was certain she would have business. Street traffic would have to account for most of it to begin with but without a doubt the clientele would grow. Especially once she got the gowns made for Nellie. When the wives of Blake's business associates saw Nellie in Cora's dresses, she was sure they would come around to have their own creations made.

Cora wouldn't be ready to open her shop for a couple of weeks. The men carried her trunks upstairs and set one in the living room and the other in the bedroom. Afterward, she told both Asa and Harry she would be concentrating on the shop and wouldn't be going on any more outings for a while.

Again she was disappointed in Harry.

"But Cora, you have to come have dinner at my home on Sunday. Mother would like to make amends."

Have to? Cora shook her head. "I'm not ready to see your mother. To be honest, I don't like her very well and may never want to see her."

Harry took her hand. "Please. Once you get to know her, you'll love her. Everyone does."

She extracted her hand from Harry's. "I do *not* believe that to be true." *She's a manipulator and harridan and I'll be damned before I go see her again anytime soon.* "I can't believe anyone who really knows your mother would be in the least likely to like her much less love her. I'm sorry Harry, but your mother is *not* my cup of tea. Perhaps when I've gotten over her belligerence at our last meeting, I'll agree to try again."

Harry frowned. "We'll wait for now but you need to get to know Mother, at some point or another."

"Hmpft. We'll see." *I don't know if I want to take on a mother-in-law like her especially living with us. I like Harry but am*

I ready for that?

She cooked her favorite meal while they moved her belongings. She unpacked some of her mother's china to use for dinner, the others she'd put in the cupboards above the sink after the men were gone.

Cora fixed a roast beef with Yorkshire pudding, mashed potatoes, gravy, asparagus, biscuits and a cherry cobbler for desert. "All right gentlemen, dinner is served. Please help yourselves."

The table was round so neither man sat any farther away from Cora than the other. And they were a determined lot, inching closer to her every time they got up to get food from the counter where she had laid it out, and then sat again, which was more often than necessary. At last, Cora slapped her napkin on the table. "Will you two stop this? Sit in your seats and do not rise again until dinner is over. I'm disappointed in you both. Playing nonsense games like this. I appreciate that each of you wants to be close to me, but really. Are you children?"

"No" Asa and Harry said at the same time.

Asa placed his hand over hers. "I'm sorry, Cora. I don't know what's gotten into me."

"That's all right, Asa." She looked over at Harry who'd just put another bite of roast in his mouth. Without prodding he was not going to apologize. She stared at him.

"Well, Harry? Are you, too, sorry for being boorish?"

He swallowed quickly. "Um, yes. Yes of course I apologize, m'dear."

Maybe I am being too hard on poor Harry, but he lied, all right not lied but definitely omitted. And his mother is a huge omission.

Once dinner was over, Cora wished both men good night and went about the business of unpacking her trunks. She started with the two upstairs, one with her clothing and the other her hope chest.

Until tonight before dinner, she hadn't opened her hope chest for a long, long time. The trunk contained her mother's beautiful rose-patterned china.

The plates, bowls and cups were wrapped in her linens including embroidered sheets and pillowcases, napkins and table cloths. She had two sets of silver candlesticks and a full set of silver eating and serving utensils.

Also in the trunk was her wedding dress. She'd designed it herself in pale pink silk, and though not in the latest style, the gown was flattering on Cora's figure. The off-the-shoulder bodice was filled with white lace from her bosom to her neck. She had no bustle, but with three petticoats underneath the skirt provided plenty of fullness. Long white gloves and a lace mantilla to cover her head completed the ensemble, much to her satisfaction.

She'd made this particular dress when she thought she'd be marrying Asa. Why did wearing that same dress to marry Harry suddenly seem so wrong? Perhaps she should put up the dress as one of her samples. No she needed samples of the latest styles out of New York and Paris. Once she got her sewing machine, there was a dealer in town, she could have several sample dresses done in no time. She'd make them with large enough seams and without hems so the alterations would be easy for any women, regardless their size.

Cora finished unpacking her hope chest and moved on to her wardrobe. She'd brought only the newest and most flattering of her clothes. Her parents were wealthy and indulged her desire to be a seamstress. The money they provided had allowed her to work as a seamstress, though she never had enough until now, to open her own shop. She enjoyed making clothes for herself and others. She'd donated most of her clothing to the church for their poor before she started her adventure to San Francisco. Her allowance from her parents allowed her to buy material where most women who worked with her could not. She'd have no trouble replacing the clothing she'd given away.

Taking the sleeves off one pattern and mix those with the bodice from another, and the skirt from yet another to make the most flattering design, was not unusual for Cora. She liked to sew and create.

Once she was done putting her clothes away in the wardrobe and the closet, she made tea. Taking the cup of hot brew with her she walked downstairs to work on her trunks with the sewing supplies, pattern books and material. She had twenty full bolts of cloth. Cottons, satins, silks, wools and velvets. She could make everything from a chemise to an evening gown to a man's suit, although she doubted any man would come to her shop. San Francisco surely had plenty of tailors for men to choose from.

The sale of her parent's home had brought Cora thirty-eight thousand dollars. Her parents had thought she and her brother were smart enough not to need an executer to see to the will and the money their deaths would bring to their children. Cora ended up with Virgil's share as well, since he hadn't been married at the time of his death.

It was a large home on a good sized piece of ground on New York's Long Island and had sold quickly. She wondered now if she had asked enough for it, but she'd been ready to sell and got the price she asked.

She stacked the material along a wide shelf in the sewing room made especially for the bolts with small pieces of wood about six inches tall every one to two feet or so, forming long slots along the shelf to separate the bolts. Each bolt held between forty and one hundred yards of material. She sorted the cloth by type, putting all cottons together, then the silks, satins, wools and last the bolts of velvet she'd brought. She planned on having more than one hundred bolts of cloth eventually. Lots of variety for the clients to choose from.

Her cloth was a large investment. The bolts each cost her a pretty penny and together represented almost ten thousand dollars. She'd saved for years to buy material and even used part of the money from the sale of her house to buy the cloth. The cottons ran about one hundred dollars per bolt and the silks and velvets could be more than one thousand dollars depending on the pattern in the cloth. She had one emerald silk that had a border of roses done with silver thread. It was spectacular and would make a glorious skirt for a ball gown.

Her first purchase would be a good sewing machine, one with a sturdy treadle and heavy duty needles. The machine would cost her one hundred and twenty-five dollars but it would be worth every penny. She could make five garments in the same amount of time in which she used to make one and still have the quality she wanted to maintain. If she was smart she'd buy two machines now and plan on hiring a girl to sew sooner rather than later. Another thing to talk to Blake and Nellie about. She was compiling quite a list for them.

*****

With Nellie in mind, her first creation would be an evening gown from the emerald silk. The bodice, fitted to Nellie like a corset, would include stays to give it shape, and then give way to a full skirt and draped bustle. The bottom edge of the material was embroidered with a rose pattern in silver thread and looked spectacular. There were tiny, puffed sleeves and she'd make gloves to match rather than the standard white gloves that most ladies wore with their evening gowns. The dress would look amazing on Nellie with her pale blond hair and green eyes.

She spread the fabric on the cutting table and got out her pattern books. With the utmost care she laid out the pattern pieces, made of durable paper for more than one use, on the silk, pinned them down and then cut around them. When she was done, she folded the material with the pattern still attached. She would keep it that way until she was ready to sew the garment together.

Cora's sewing machines arrived the following week. The delivery man carried both into the back room and she tipped him five dollars. Paying a delivery fee was worth it not to have to deal with her gentlemen callers falling over each other to move the machines and breaking one or both before she got a chance to use the equipment.

Although, she really need not have worried since Harry did not come over at all in the two weeks since she'd moved in. He had sent her several messages asking her to have dinner at his house. She declined each one.

Asa came by the shop every day, ever the attentive suitor.

She spent two days sewing the emerald gown and the three other dresses she'd cut out. Now, with samples ready, she could open her shop. Her stomach did somersaults as she watched the sign painter put her name across one of the display windows. On Friday, July 26, 1867, Creations by Cora was born. This was hers, her baby and she loved it like any new mother.

Asa was there with her to celebrate when she turned over the 'open' sign. She wondered how he managed to continue to stay in San Francisco with her. He'd told her he 'was not without funds' so he must be using all of his savings and that bothered her, but in the end it was his money to do with as he pleased.

Blake and Nellie and their children would be over later in the evening for an opening party. She was suddenly concerned with her sanity, planning a party for tonight. Taking a deep breath, she realized that whatever she managed to do for food and drink would be fine. These were her friends. They, of all people, would understand.

Harry was supposed to come to the shop today. She'd sent him word by messenger that she would be open for business and was having a celebration that evening.

"Cora," Asa wrapped his arms around her from behind. "Why don't you just marry me? You know I'll do anything for you."

She pulled out of his arms and turned. "I know you think that now, but part of me still wonders if you'll be there when the times get tough."

He sighed. "I know I don't deserve your trust, but I hope that I'm building your faith in me by being here for you. I intend to always be here for you, Cora. I want to spend my life with you. What more can I do to prove it?"

"Just continue to be there for me, Asa." She wrapped her arms around his neck and lightly kissed his lips. They were soft and she pressed hers more firmly against them. She broke the kiss, her breathing slightly ragged. It was nice, very nice to kiss Asa. "I need to have someone I can count on. You, Nellie and Annie are the only friends I have here in San Francisco."

"Uh Hmm." Someone cleared their throat behind Asa.

She looked over Asa's shoulder and saw Harry, standing in the doorway between the sewing room and the show room.

Watching, she saw Harry clench his teeth, a vein in his forehead throbbed, and he was red with anger. "Am I interrupting something?"

Aside from the anger, she heard the hurt and jealousy in his voice and immediately guilt assaulted her.

"Oh, Harry," She stepped quickly away from Asa. "I wasn't expecting you until this evening after you got off work."

"I can see that. I thought I'd drop by early and bring you lunch." He held up the basket in his right hand.

Cora walked forward and took the container. "How sweet of you. And I admit, totally unexpected." She smiled at him. "I like that."

Harry grinned wide, anger forgotten, gathered his lapels in his hands, then rocked on his heels, clearly happy with her words.

"Let's see what we have here. Fried chicken, dinner rolls, cheese, apples and wine. And there appears to be enough for three. How kind of you, Harry."

Asa smiled and winked at her.

Cora smiled, her cheeks hot, because she wanted more. More kisses, just more.

Harry's smile faded. "Hmpft."

"Come." She led the way to the little table she kept for eating in the back of the sewing room. She never went far while she ate. The table's sides folded up or down depending on what was needed. Today, she folded up one side. That gave them enough room for three.

"Asa, would you bring over the chair from the one of the sewing machines, please?"

"Sure."

He walked over, his limp a little more pronounced today than it had been.

She wanted to ask him about it but not in front of Harry. Cora wondered if the San Francisco climate, with the dampness off the ocean, was affecting his leg, perhaps making his knee hurt. But he didn't mention any pain, so she wouldn't either—at least for now.

While they ate and chatted, she couldn't help but notice having both Harry and Asa there for meals was nice. But she knew she needed to make a decision about which one she would marry...if either. Both men tried to be solicitous of her feelings and to cater to her every whim. Asa was better at it, but then, he did know her better having been her friend since she was a child.

Why was she thinking about these things now, while they ate and she needed to pay strict attention?

Harry was trying harder and he hadn't mentioned his mother lately, but the woman was forever in the background. Cora knew if she married Harry, he'd expect his mother to live with them. That thought sent shivers up her spine. There was still something untoward about that relationship, something which made Cora uneasy. More than the fact that she didn't like the old biddy.

When they finished their meal, Cora scraped the dishes, stacked them and put them to the side of the stairs leading up to her apartment above the shop. She would take them upstairs and wash them later, before going to bed.

"I need to get to work now gentlemen. Thank you both for being here on my first day open, but I have dresses to sew." She waved them both toward the door. "I'm trying my hand at original designs, rather than those I get out of a pattern book. If I sew up a couple of samples, I'm hopeful that ladies will want what they see. I'll see you both tonight at the party. It'll be just a very small get together with my friends. Harry?"

"Yes, m'dear."

"Do *not* bring your mother. She is not welcome."

"I understand. I'll see you tonight. Alone."

"Good. See you then."

"I wish you the best of luck today." Asa came forward and she raised her cheek for him to kiss, which he did tenderly. He then took her hand, turned it over and kissed the inside of her wrist, and then licked it.

Her eyes slammed wide open.

"Until tonight, sweet Cora." He whispered, his breath soft over her lips.

Oh my! Her heart turned over. She gazed into the cobalt blue of his eyes and saw a twinkle there she hadn't seen since before he went off to the war. She longed to ask him what mischief he was up to, but with Harry there she couldn't.

Harry came forward and she raised her other cheek to him. Instead of kissing her as Asa had done, he put his knuckle under her chin and turned her head until she faced him. Then he slanted his lips over hers in a gentle, searing kiss.

"Until tonight, Cora."

The men walked out together, neither wanting to leave the other behind with her.

She moved the chair back to the sewing machine and sat to put together the dress she'd cut out that morning, but found herself thinking instead of the two men who'd just left.

Harry's kiss was unexpected and very nice. She admitted she'd wanted more, but he'd pulled away.

Asa's kiss before Harry had come in showed great promise as well. She was beginning to wonder if she wasn't some sort of strumpet, wanting to enjoy more kisses from both men. But the kiss on her wrist, followed by his tongue had taken her breath away and made hot liquid pool in her groin.

She wanted to know more of what that was about.

There was Asa, with his graying brown hair, that she found herself oddly attracted to and Harry, his wavy blond hair, slicked back so the curls wouldn't show. Both seemed to be good, decent men. She knew for sure Asa was and Harry was trying to be pleasant and though he was not very attentive.

Asa treated her well. Harry tried in his own way but he had lied to her, taken her to a terrible restaurant and had witch for a mother. But he is likable. Both want to marry her.

How was she going to choose? Or had she already made her choice and simply didn't want to face telling them?

CHAPTER 7

Nearly two months had passed since that dreadful dinner with Henrietta Belcher. Cora refused to go back to Harry's or to deal with the woman, even though he kept asking. She was not ready to put herself back in that situation. Yet, how can she keep that up if she is seriously considering Harry as husband material?

The bell above the door sounded and brought her out of her reverie.

"Be right there," Cora called from the sewing room. She checked her appearance in the mirror before walking out front. "How may I help you?"

The woman turned to face Cora. "Quite a nice shop you have here, my dear."

Cora sucked in a breath and cocked an

eyebrow. "Henrietta. How surprising to see you here."

Harry's mother nonchalantly waved her hand and then began removing her gloves. "Nonsense. You haven't been back to the house, so I have to come to you. I want to apologize for my awful behavior when you were there. I thought I could bully you as I have...well, never mind. Needless to say, you were not to be bullied."

Cora crossed her arms over her chest. "No. I won't be bullied."

"And you probably won't take well to being threatened either."

Cora narrowed her eyes. "No. I don't like threats."

"Then I won't threaten you, but I will make you a promise. You will marry my son or this beautiful little shop you've put so much work into will suddenly be engulfed in flames. The whole building and anyone unlucky enough to be in it. Do you understand my meaning?"

"I understand quite well." Cora put her shoulders back and straightened to her full height. She approached the woman, who was taller than Cora by several inches. She poked Henrietta in the chest with her finger.

Her fear of the woman, replaced by anger. "I won't be threatened. You can tell Harry that there is no way on God's green earth that I would marry him now, knowing what a harridan he has for a mother. It's too bad really, as I think I was leaning in Harry's direction. Now leave my shop and don't ever come back."

Henrietta face lost its color and she swallowed hard. The look on her face when Cora said she'd been leaning in Harry's direction was the best revenge,

"Perhaps I've misjudged you," she said quickly, licking lips. "Can't you and Harry continue as though I never was here?"

Cora laughed but there was nothing joyful in the sound. "No. It's done. Harry and I are through. He was to take me to the opera tonight. If he comes here, I will send him away and tell him exactly why. You, Henrietta," she crossed her arms over her chest. "will have to deal with your son's temper and I'm sure he has one. I've almost seen it on several occasions, but he's very good at keeping that side of him reined in. I have a feeling he'll unleash it for you. Now leave my shop before I throw you out."

Lips pressed into a tight line, Henrietta

put on her gloves. "This isn't over, Cora. Not by any means."

"Yes. It is. Please leave." She pointed at the exit. "Don't let the door slam on your way out."

The old woman walked out, back ramrod straight, head high.

Cora shook with both anger and fear. What in the world was going on? Why was it so important that she marry Harry? Important enough that his mother would threaten her with harm? She walked to the door, flipped the sign over and turned the key in the lock. Cora needed some tea and a few minutes to calm down and stop shaking. It's not like people were beating down her door to get in, anyway.

She ran upstairs, set the kettle to boil and got a cup and saucer from the cupboard. From her trembling hands the cup clattered onto the saucer. She placed her hands on the counter and leaned there, taking a moment to gather herself together. She would not let this woman frighten her.

An hour later, Cora was calmer *and* she was resolved. Her first thought was to marry Asa right away, but it was unfair to use him to avoid being forced to marry Harry. No.

Cora must tell Harry what had happened and that she was done with him. If he couldn't control his mother before they had married, what would their life have been like after? She refused to live like that...live in fear of making her mother-in-law unhappy.

Pounding sounded on the door downstairs. She put her teacup in the sink and went down to reopen the store.

When she walked through the doorway from the sewing room to the show room, she saw the person at the door was Harry. Her heart jumped and her stomach churned. Taking a deep breath, she put her hand on her stomach, then walked forward, turned over the sign to open, unlocked the door and opened it.

"Harry. I hadn't expected you so soon, although I suppose I should have if you have talked to your mother."

He followed her inside the store. "What does my mother have to do with anything?"

"She was just here about an hour ago and threatened me with harm. I might as well tell you now, I will *not* be marrying you Harry." She lifted her chin and crossed her arms over her chest. "As a matter of fact, I don't want to see you again. Your mother is dangerous and you need to control her now. My Lord, imagine what would have happened after we were married. No, I will not put up with that. Goodbye, Harry. Please leave."

"No. Cora, let me talk to her." Harry grabbed her arm and stopped her from stepping away from him.

She looked down at where he held her. "Let me go."

Instead he pulled her to him wrapping her tightly in his arms. "I know you feel something for me. I could tell by the way you responded when we kissed."

"No. Harry. There is nothing between us. My response to your kiss was simply one of surprise. Nothing more."

Lowering his head, he pressed his lips against hers.

The bell above the door sounded.

She turned her head to the side and pushed with her trapped arms. "No!"

"Leave her alone!"

Cora recognized Asa's voice and she sagged in Harry's arms, her legs weak. Asa was here. He would save her.

Asa put a hand on Harry's shoulder and pulled him backward.

Harry turned to face Asa. "Why don't *you* leave, cripple, and let us be?"

"No, Harry. You need to leave and not return." Asa held out his arm to Cora.

Relief flooded her body and she flew to his side, sliding behind him.

Harry's lips thinned to a flat line. "All right I'm leaving, but I'll be back. We have to discuss this, Cora."

Catching her breath, Cora came from behind Asa and stood next to him. "There is nothing to discuss. I don't want to see you again. You and your mother have harassed me, threatened me and taken advantage of me for the last time."

"Leave, Belcher, while you still can." Asa moved himself between Harry and Cora.

"For now." Harry turned and stalked out of the shop.

Asa turned to Cora. "Are you all right? Did he hurt you?"

She moved into his arms, into the safety his embrace provided and was wrapped in his warmth. "His mother came by earlier and threatened to burn down the shop if I didn't marry Harry and then he came and...and." Tears rolled down her cheeks and she sniffled. "Oh, Asa, I don't know what would have happened if you hadn't come when you did."

He hugged her closer. "We won't think about that. You're safe. I'm here and I won't let anything happen to you."

*****

Harry stalked through the front door of the mansion, slamming it behind him. Jenkins, the butler, took one look at him and turned, heading back toward the kitchen.

"Mother!"

He strode directly to the library and wrenched open the door.

"Harry. Do stop going on so. You'll scare the servants."

Henrietta Belcher sat on the settee, a snifter of whiskey in one hand and a cheroot in the other.

"I thought I told you not to smoke in here," Harry growled on his way to the sidebar to pour himself three, maybe even four, fingers of Jameson Irish. Jameson was the best whiskey to be had in San Francisco, perhaps the world, and the only whiskey allowed in the Belcher house. His mother drank only the best.

"And I thought I made it clear, this is *my*

home. You are a visitor here and I'll smoke where I like. I agreed not to smoke outside of the house but that is the only concession you have from me."

"So, I know why I'm drinking in the middle of the day. Tell me why you are."

Henrietta took a large swallow of the amber brown liquid. "I made a huge mistake today. I threatened Cora." She stopped, her hand shaking a little and she took another sip of the drink.

"Go on. What did you threaten? I already know you were there."

"I told her if," she swallowed hard, then rushed on. "If she didn't marry you, I'd burn down her shop and I implied she would be in the building at the time."

His jaw dropped for a moment. "Good Lord, Mother. What were you thinking? No wonder she doesn't want to see me again. I think we've lost her. We'll have to start over."

"No. I must have a grandchild. You know I don't have much time, and I need one before I die. I'm not leaving this estate to you. You'll gamble it away. If I don't have a grandchild, the church will get all but a minor portion that I will settle on you. I will leave you the house, how you keep it or if you sell it is up to you. But that will be your inheritance…unless there is a grandchild. Do you understand the importance of this to me?"

"Yes, Mother." He sighed. "I understand. The situation is just as important to me. I don't want to be left a pauper. You know I'd have to sell the house. I don't make enough money to keep up the house and indulge in my pastimes."

"Then you better find a way to get that girl to marry you and give you a child. Time is running out Harry."

Henrietta took another puff of her cheroot and suddenly had a coughing fit. She put down the cigar in the ashtray at her side. Then took the hanky from her sleeve, and spat blood into the cloth. "Do you see? I'm running out of time…and so are you." She folded the cloth and set it on the table next to the ashtray.

Harry took a deep breath. "Yes, Mother. I'll find a solution to our problems. Very soon."

She nodded, took a drink of the whiskey and picked up her smoking stub.

He swallowed the remainder of the drink

in his glass, put it on the counter and filled it with another measure of the beautiful golden liquid.

"Cora will marry me. She'll have to. I'll see to it."

"That's my boy."

*****

Hours later, Cora turned over the sign so it read 'closed' and then locked the door. "Asa, would you stay for dinner? I'm not ready to be alone. I should be worried about my reputation, but right now, I don't care. My reputation or my life? I choose my life."

"Of course. If there is ever a word said about your character, I'll set them straight. You are after all still my fiancée." He stroked her cheek, his touch light as a feather upon her face. "You don't have to ask for my help. I'm here for you whenever you want me."

She closed her eyes and leaned into his hand. Safe. He made her feel safe. Cora led the way up the stairs to her apartment. "I'm afraid I was just planning on having bacon and eggs for dinner. Will that be all right?"

He grinned. "Perfect. I love breakfast for dinner."

Cora nodded her head and smiled. "So

do I. It's my favorite meal."

"Another thing we have in common. We like a lot of the same things don't you think?"

"I suppose we do. We grew up together."

Asa sat at the table with a cup of cold coffee while Cora prepared their dinner.

"Can I tell you a secret?" He'd taken a coin out of his pocket and was twirling it in and out of his fingers.

"Certainly. Is it a good secret?" She cut the bacon slab into thick slices and put the strips into the cast iron skillet to fry.

"I think so."

"Very well, what is it?"

He stopped playing with the coin. "I never thought you were tagging along. I always liked having you with us. When you were small, watching you trying to do the same things we did, was very entertaining. Then when you got out of the schoolroom, and turned into this beautiful woman, I was afraid you'd marry and leave...me."

Cora placed her hands on the counter and looked skyward. "But I didn't marry. The war started and all the young men left."

"A lot of them married before they left. I

asked you to marry me because I couldn't stand the thought of you belonging to another man. I wanted you for my own, even then."

Cora stopped fixing dinner and turned to face Asa, feeling the pain, caused by his words. "If you wanted me so much, why didn't you come home to me? I could have dealt with anything but the betrayal is still hard to tolerate. I want you to understand something, too. Just because I've told Harry I don't want to see him ever again, doesn't mean I'm marrying you. We still have issues we need to work through."

"I understand. I did hope that my suit might be looked upon more favorably now."

"I've always looked favorably on you, Asa. That's why I agreed to marry you in the first place."

He stood and walked to her. "But you didn't love me."

She looked up into his beautiful blue eyes surrounded by thick dark brown lashes. He had little creases beside them she hadn't noticed before. The lines added character. "I don't know what I felt for you. Whatever it may have been was over shadowed by your death and my grieving your loss. I still have a hard time believing you're really here and going to stay."

Asa touched his fingers to her temple and pulled them slowly down her jaw until he cupped her face with his palm. "I'm not leaving, Cora, I promise you. I don't ever want to hurt you again. You mean the world to me." He lowered his head and his lips claimed hers. He slanted his mouth over hers, drinking from her. His tongue pressed against her lips begging for entrance.

She granted it, relishing the flavor of him. Coffee and the sugar cookies she'd set on the table when he first sat. Slowly, the kiss gentled and he pulled away.

Cora was out of breath, and glad to see Asa was as affected as she was. She blinked several times and swallowed hard, surprised to find her arms wrapped around his neck. "Well. That's definitely something new. You've never kissed me like that before."

"I wanted to show you all that I feel in my heart. I love you, Cora."

She unwrapped her arms. "Please don't say that. I can't return the sentiment to you, not yet. I care for you, Asa, but a great shadow is over us. Please don't try to push me."

"I don't want to push you." He slowly pulled his arms from around her to rest at his sides. "But I won't easily let you go, either. I made that mistake once, and it nearly cost me everything I hold dear. I won't let that happen again."

Cora lifted her hand and brought the backs of her fingers down his jaw feeling the whiskers that were already growing back since his morning shave. "Let's just take it a day at a time and see where it takes us."

"As long as I can see you every single day, that's fine with me."

She laughed. "Are you sure you want to see me that often? You may get tired of me."

His mouth quirked up in a small grin. "Never. I'll never tire of seeing your beautiful face."

She smiled and let out a sigh. "You do know what to say to make a girl happy."

"The only girl I care about is you."

Cora suddenly smelled acrid smoke and glanced toward the stove. "The bacon."

The pan was spewing smoke into the room. She grabbed a pot holder and pulled the skillet off the burner and set it in the sink.

She sighed. "Looks like it's just eggs

tonight."

"Nonsense." Asa doused the fire under the burner. "I'm taking you to dinner. Where would you like to go?"

"Out? But I…"

"Never mind what we were going to do, this works out perfectly. I love showing you off to the world. I want everyone to know what a lucky man I am."

"All right. You do flatter me so." She smiled, relieved the situation was thwarted. "I know this will sound strange, but I'd like to go back to the hotel restaurant where we first had dinner. It was such a wonderful night and the food was good, too."

"The Golden State Hotel it is. Get your wrap and let's go."

"Let me check my hair and—"

He grabbed her hand. "Trust me. You look beautiful."

Cora smiled and squeezed his hand. "All right. Let's go to dinner."

CHAPTER 8

Harry stood in the shadows on the corner across the street from Cora's shop. Asa had stayed with her all day which hadn't given Harry a chance to talk to her. He held one of his mother's cheroots in one hand. Even though he didn't like the things, smoking gave him something to do for the long hours he waited to get Cora alone.

He watched Asa come out and thought, now was his chance, but then he saw Cora follow him and knew they were going to dinner. No point in waiting here any longer. There was no telling how long they would be gone.

A pang of regret tore through him. He and Cora were supposed to go to the opera tonight. He had planned to ask her again to marry him. If his mother had only waited… He felt sure Cora would have chosen him. She'd told his mother she was leaning toward him…until all this happened. Now he'd have to force her to marry him. He didn't like the thought of doing that to Cora. He really did care for her, but she had to marry him, she had to bear him a child. The marriage was the only way he could continue living the lifestyle to which he'd become accustomed. But he was running out of time.

*****

Cora and Asa returned to her store after their dinner at the Golden State Hotel restaurant. After they got out of the cab, Asa paid the driver, took Cora's arm and escorted her to the door.

"Asa! Look! My door."

The glass in her door was shattered. She quickly unlocked the door and was about to enter.

Asa stopped her.

"Let me go first."

Once across the threshold, he looked down,

She followed his gaze. A brick was just inside, lying on the broken glass, a note tied to the stone.

Crouching, Asa carefully cut the string with his pocket knife and handed the letter to Cora.

She unfolded the paper and quickly read it.

This is your last warning. You know what must be done. Your decision will determine if there is a next time and if there is, the damage won't be from a brick through your window.

H

"It's her. It's Henrietta. She warned me she'd burn my shop down if I didn't marry Harry."

Asa took the paper from her and read it for himself. He frowned and crumpled the note in his hand. "You're not marrying Harry. You can't seriously be considering it after this? What if the H stands for Harry not Henrietta? Could he be behind this and not his mother?"

Cora picked her way through the shards of glass and walked back to the sewing room to get a broom and dust pan. "I don't know. He doesn't really seem capable of this kind of behavior whereas his mother is totally capable. She's insane. Absolutely insane and will stop at nothing if it gets her what she wants...namely for me to bear Harry a child."

Asa shook his head. "Seems like a lot of trouble to go through just to get Harry a son or daughter."

She gathered her tools and walked back up front, with Asa following her with the wastebasket. "It's not for Harry, it's for her. She wants the child. I don't think Harry cares one way or the other. At least he doesn't seem to."

The glass had exploded upon impact from the brick and was everywhere. Thank goodness her samples were in the picture windows and behind the brick. All the glass went forward into the room, not backward into her dresses.

When she finally got up the last piece of sparkling remains she could see, they returned to the work room. Cora didn't have any wood to cover the hole in the door, but she did have some heavy cotton she'd brought for dresses for the staff of some of her wealthier shop patrons. She cut the material to fit the opening, and Asa nailed it to the door.

Cora admired their handiwork. "I think

that's the best that can be done for tonight."

"Anyone could come in. You can't stay here. Come back to the hotel with me."

"I can't stay there." She shook her head. "Doing so would be unseemly and what if one of my clients saw me? No. I'll be fine here."

"Then I'm staying with you. I'm not going to let you remain alone."

"Well, I don't know…" She crossed her arms over her nervous stomach.

"It's settled. I'll sleep on your sofa."

"Fine." She let out a sigh. "I don't really want to be alone, anyway. I'm scared, Asa. What if she decides that if Harry can't have me, no one will? She's capable of doing me great harm, I think even murder."

Asa wrapped her in his arms again and she felt safe once more.

"I won't let anything happen to you. Not now, not ever. I will always be here for you. Please try to believe me. I won't leave you again, Cora."

He raised her chin with his knuckle until she looked at him. "Trust me." His lips touched hers, and he sipped from her like she was a fine wine.

She craved his touch and wound her

arms around his neck, drinking from him as he did from her.

*****

Cora waited until Asa left then she walked to Main Street and caught a cab to Blake and Nellie's.

Upon her arrival, James, the butler, took her coat and showed her immediately to the library.

"I believe you are expected, Miss Jones."

Before she could respond, James opened the door to the library and ushered her through.

Blake saw her, stood and came forward to greet her.

"Cora. I see you got my message. I'm very glad you were able to come alone." He took her hand and placed it in the crook of his elbow for the short distance to the settee where Nellie waited.

Nellie patted the seat next to her. "Come sit by me."

Blake guided Cora to the sofa.

"So, what did you find out?" She smoothed her skirt behind her as she sat.

"Well, Harry is the president of the bank, like he told you. He is also well-known at some of the betting parlors around town. Because he consistently loses, he is one of their favorite customers. We're talking thousands of dollars."

"I knew something was wrong." Relief poured through her. She'd been right, something was off with Harry.

Blake went to the sidebar and poured himself two fingers of amber liquid from the decanter. "There's more."

"Please go on."

"Would you like something a little stronger than the tea Nellie ordered for you?" He pointed at the bottle of liquid the color of strong tea.

"Do I need it?"

Blake held up his glass. "What do you think?"

Cora took a deep breath. "Then I suppose I better."

He poured more of the golden beverage into a glass and joined the ladies. After he gave Cora her drink, he sat in the leather chair across from them, in front of the cold fireplace.

"His mother, Henrietta Belcher, owns the house and controls the money. Harry doesn't have any of his own."

"I knew it," interrupted Cora, feeling a knot grow in her stomach. "He took me to that awful oyster shack for our first dinner out, said it was one of his favorites. Now, I think he was just trying to save money so he could go bet with it. His mother probably gave him a certain amount of money to spend on dinner."

Blake nodded. "Quite possibly."

"What else have you found out? Your tone sounded like you learned something direr than the fact he lives under his mother's thumb."

He took a deep breath. "I discovered Harry has been married before."

"What?" Her head jerked up. "That's impossible. He would have told me or Mrs. Selby would have told me."

"Actually, he's been married three times before."

"Three!" She slumped against the back of the settee.

"Yes and all of his wives have died mysteriously by some accident. The first one was hit by a carriage while shopping downtown. The second fell down the stairs in the house and the third fell asleep in the bathtub and drowned."

Brows drawn into a frown, she looked between Nellie and Blake. "Harry's only thirty-five. He can't have been married long to any of those poor women."

"According to my sources each marriage lasted about two years before each wife died," confirmed Blake.

Nellie, who had been quiet up until now, asked the burning question. "Don't you think it's too much of a coincidence that each of his wives died in an accident when they'd been married about two years? Do you think they were murdered?"

Cora sat up straight, gasped and her hand flew to her throat. "Oh, dear. I hope you're wrong. If not, I could have been marrying a murderer and probably been his next victim."

"You should be very careful when you are around Harry." Blake took a sip of his drink. "He may have had nothing to do with the deaths of those women. But if he did, he may not easily take no for an answer."

Cora downed her drink in one gulp and the whiskey burned all the way down. "I think I need another one." She held up her glass for Blake to take.

He got her another two fingers of

whiskey and returned the glass.

She sipped this one, still reeling from the fire the last one caused in her belly. Cora leaned back on the sofa and closed her eyes. All she saw were the blank faces of three murdered women. Was she supposed to be the next? What if she was wrong and it was only coincidence that all three women had died? She'd be wrong to accuse Harry of that. Did she want to take the chance? Did she care enough about Harry to take the risk?

The short answer was 'no'. She was interested in Harry from his letters but in the flesh he'd been a big disappointment. But with Asa it was different. She cared deeply for Asa and the more she was with him, the more she was sure he was the one she would marry. She might even love him, but she wasn't sure she knew what love felt like.

"What are you going to do?" Nellie placed her hand on Cora's leg. "You're not serious about marrying Harry are you? Not after these revelations. Are you?"

Slowly, Cora shook her head. "Even before all this came out I was pretty sure I wasn't marrying Harry. For one thing, I can't stand his mother. The woman is intolerable. If anyone could have murdered those women, Henrietta is the first person I would suspect. Besides after I heard her threat, I told Harry I wouldn't marry him."

Nellie's eyes widened and she leaned forward. "She threatened you?"

"Yes." Cora nodded. "She said if I didn't marry Harry she'd burn down the building and hinted that I'd be in it at the time. I'm still afraid to be on my own, but I can't have Asa there all the time."

"Oh, my God, Cora. You need to go to the police." Nellie took Cora's hand in hers. "Tell them what happened."

Blake shook his head. "It wouldn't do any good. She'd be looked at as a disgruntled mail-order bride making accusations against a prominent member of society. It would be thrown out and would irrevocably damage Cora's business. No society lady would cross the threshold."

Cora nodded. "That's true and the more I think about it the more I believe the note was from Henrietta. It had to be."

Blake sat back in the leather chair across from her and Nellie. "You're probably right since she's the one who holds the purse strings. Harry's liable to do whatever the old woman wants."

Cora nodded. "You wouldn't believe what she's like. She kept insisting that I marry Harry, and whatever I said made no difference to her. She just kept saying I would end up making that decision. That I would fall in love with her son. And Harry keeps saying I'll love his mother when I get to know her, that everyone does. Whenever I hear someone say something like that 'everyone does', I automatically assume the opposite. In this case, I can't see how anyone would like her much less love that despicable, nasty..." She waved a hand and shook her head. "Sorry, I'm letting my emotions get the best of me."

"Whatever you decide to do," said Blake as he leaned forward. "I wouldn't let myself be alone with Harry in the future. Stay at the shop or go out to restaurants and include Asa every time."

Cora took another sip of her liquor. "What am I to do if Harry is like his mother and won't take 'no' for an answer?"

They were all quiet for the moment. No one seemed to know the answer to that.

"Then you'll have to marry Asa," said Blake. "If there is any chance that you could change your mind, Harry is likely to take advantage of it."

Cora smiled. "I think I've wanted to marry Asa all along, but I was so hurt and angry I couldn't admit it. I was thrilled he wasn't dead, and even more so that he would come all this way to marry me when I could have already been married to Harry for all he knew."

Nellie looked up at Blake and smiled. "If you'd acted like we did, you would be married to Harry now."

"That's true, you two didn't wait at all, but your relationship seems to be working out."

Nellie blushed.

Blake looked at Nellie and chuckled. "It does, doesn't it? Nellie and I both felt the same way and knew getting married was what we wanted. You have to do what you think is best. If that means you marry Harry, so be it, but in my opinion, based on these new findings, you would be making a grave mistake."

Cora shook her head. "I have no intention of marrying Harry. Even without this new information, I couldn't have put up with his mother. There was no way I was marrying him and I told him so. Thank you both so much for your help. I don't know what I would do if you weren't here to talk to."

"Think nothing of it, Cora," said Blake with a wave of his hand. "I'm glad to help."

Cora stood. "I should be getting home. Work does come early."

"I'll have the carriage brought to the front." Blake went to the bell cord and pulled.

James entered the room a few minutes later. "Yes, sir. How can I be of service?"

"Have Otis bring around the carriage to take Miss Jones home."

"Yes, sir." James nodded and left the room.

Cora downed the last of her drink and set the glass on the table. She swayed a little and had to sit again.

"Are you sure you don't want to stay here tonight?" asked Nellie, concern laced her voice.

"No, I'll be fine. Otis will see me home."

*****

Cora hadn't seen Harry for two weeks. She stopped brushing her hair in preparation for the day and put down the hairbrush on the vanity table. Had it really been two weeks? She and Asa spent every waking minute together. He sat at the table in the sewing room and read while she worked. Almost daily, he made lunch and brought it down to her, so they could eat at the table together. He hadn't let her cook since the night of the smoking bacon, but instead he took her to a different restaurant every night.

She put her hair up in a bun at the base of her neck and went downstairs. Pulling the skirt she'd cut out yesterday from the pile of material at the end of the cutting table, she laid it out. The bell above the door sounded and Cora didn't even bother to look up from the skirt she was sewing. "Good morning, Asa."

"Not Asa I'm afraid, my dear."

Hearing the voice made Cora shake and she stopped pushing the sewing machine's treadle with her feet. The needle immediately stopped moving.

She turned to face the intruder. Was he drunk, coming here like this? He didn't appear to be. "Harry. What are you doing here?"

"No need to fear me, my dear. I've just

come to talk."

"We have nothing to talk about."

"Oh, but we do."

"Asa will be here soon."

"I brought a special sign and locked the door. He'll think you went to the bank and won't be back for a little while."

Cora's heart pounded so hard in her chest, she expected the organ to punch its way out of her body at any moment. She stood, taking her scissors with her and hiding them in the pocket of her skirt. "What do you want, Harry?"

"Just to talk, uninterrupted, for a few minutes. That's all. I promise." He crossed his heart.

"Come back and sit at the table. There's a pot of coffee though it's no longer hot."

He waved his arm and shook his head. "I don't need any coffee."

They walked back to the table and sat across from each other.

"I'm sorry for all the distress my mother caused you. She didn't mean what she said. She only wanted to scare you into marrying me." He hung his head for a moment. "She feels awful."

"Hmpft. She only feels awful because it

backfired on her. I didn't acquiesce to her demands but went totally against them. Then she had a brick thrown through my window with a note that basically said she'd murder me if I didn't marry you."

"I'm so sorry. But I want you to ignore my mother. I know that you were beginning to have some feelings for me. Are those all gone?"

She hesitated, remembering his letters, his humorous anecdotes. Surely there was still that part of Harry here.

Harry relaxed against the back of the chair. "They aren't. Thank God. I was afraid you would hate me forever for what my mother had done."

"I don't hate you." Cora took her hand off the cutting shears and clasped both hands together in her lap. "Though I can't say the same for your mother. She threatened to kill me."

"She's desperate. Let me tell you a little about Mother. She was an only child, raised in a wealthy home by a nanny. She rarely saw her parents and when she did, they were usually fighting. Mother never wanted to subject herself to the same kind of relationship, so she didn't want to marry.

However, that's not how the world worked. She was required to marry, and so found someone she could at least be friends with."

Cora nodded. "Your father?"

"My father. There was never any great love between them, but they managed to be friends." He chuckled. "Luckily they were more than friends often enough for me to be conceived. I hope I'm not making you uncomfortable. I know this is not a proper subject to discuss with an unmarried young lady, like yourself."

Cora shook her head. "No, go on. I find I'm fascinated."

Harry smiled. "There were never any more children, and when my father died, my mother went crazy for a time. Now she has little time before she joins him. Probably a year, two at the most. She's determined to have a grandchild before she dies. Determined to see her legacy carried on. That's why she's so adamant I marry and have children right away."

Cora placed her hands on the table. "I'm very sorry for your mother, but that does not excuse the fact that she threatened my life and my livelihood, if I didn't marry you. No. I think it best we call a halt to this relationship before we get any further along. After hearing your mother's threats, I could never live in the same house with her. Never."

"Please Cora." Harry took her left hand in his. "Think about it. Don't say no."

She tugged on her hand but he held fast.

"Let go of my hand." She clenched her jaw. "Please."

"Cora," Harry shook his head. "Don't do this. Don't make it harder on yourself."

He's not sane either. How can he hear her denial and ignore her words? Her heart beat hammered in her chest and she was short of breath, but she would not give in to panic, instead she very calmly said, "If you don't let go of my hand now, I won't be responsible for the consequences."

Harry's eyes narrowed and his lips formed a thin line. "Listen to me, you little ingrate. I bought you. Paid to have you brought out here to marry me, and that's exactly what you'll do."

Cora had never seen him like this. She pulled the scissors out of her pocket and stabbed the hand that held her.

"Oww! What the hell!" Harry pulled his bleeding hand to his chest. "Why'd you do that?"

"You wouldn't release me. When I say 'let me go', I mean it."

Pounding on the front door reached their ears in the back room.

She shot to her feet. "That's Asa. Don't come back, Harry. You're not welcome here."

Harry stood. "You will marry me, Cora. If it's the last thing you ever do."

She held the cutting shears in her hand, pointed in his direction like a sword in front of her. "Your mother knows I don't react well to threats. That's a lesson you are well-advised to learn, too."

"Oh, I've learned my lesson." He turned and muttered.

She wasn't sure but she though he said, "and soon you'll learn yours." Her body stiffened. "What did you say?"

"Nothing." He walked to the door, his wounded hand in his pocket. "Goodbye, Cora."

"Goodbye, Harry."

Cora followed Harry until they reached the door. Then she unlocked and opened it.

Harry hurried through without so much as a word to Asa, just looked at him then lowered his head and walked past.

Asa's gaze followed Harry down the street a ways before he came inside.

Cora waited, knowing Asa wanted to make sure Harry was gone.

He finally stepped in, shut the door behind him and followed Cora to the sewing room. "What was Harry doing here?"

"He came by to see if he could change my mind about marrying him." She set the scissors on the cutting table well away from her material. She wasn't taking any chances the blood would stain the lovely cloth. She would have to clean the shears before using them again.

"I take it by his demeanor he was unsuccessful."

"Very unsuccessful." She needed to keep busy, keep her mind off of what just transpired in her shop. Her sanctuary.

Cora bent over the table and straightened the pattern on the purple silk material. This would be an evening gown. She was making it with herself in mind since her customers seemed to be few and far between, but planning ahead she would make all the seams big enough that alterations could be made.

Asa came up behind her and wrapped his arms around her waist, gently pulling her back against him.

She let herself be moved and then placed her hands on top of Asa's arms.

"What do you want to do for dinner tonight?" He teased her ear with his lips and then kissed the sensitive skin of her neck.

Cora automatically moved her head so her neck was exposed to more of his magic lips. "I can't think when you do that to me."

"I don't want you to think, I want you to feel. Know how much I want you."

Her voice was barely a whisper. "There's no mistaking that."

He turned her in his arms until she faced him, and then cradled her face in his hands and lowered his lips to hers until they almost touched.

"I love you, Cora."

"Asa," she sighed.

His lips claimed hers, urgently, tender and fierce, all things at once until there were only the two of them in the world. Nothing else existed.

Slowly, he raised his head from hers. "Now *that* was a kiss." He wrapped his arms back around her.

She let out a moan, not wanting the moment to end. "Yes." She leaned back in his arms. "*That* was a kiss."

"Cora, I—"

She placed two fingers over his lips. "Don't say anything."

He nodded and kissed the fingers she held him with, and then pulled back so he could speak. "Back to the question at hand, what do you want to do for dinner?"

"How about we stay in tonight? I have left-over roast beef and some sourdough bread. We could make sandwiches and just visit like we used to do."

"Sounds good. Anything you want to do is fine with me as long as I get to spend the time with you."

"You say, the nicest things, Mr. Woods."

"Only to you, Miss Jones."

*****

Harry kept his hand in his pocket until he got to his carriage.

"Home," he called to his driver and climbed inside.

When he had seated himself against the green velvet cushions in the conveyance, he used the lamplight to examine his hand. The bleeding had slowed to a trickle but the puncture wound was deep. If he were to see his doctor, he'd put in stitches, but Harry didn't want to explain how he'd gotten such a wound. Instead he wrapped his hand in his handkerchief until he got home.

Once he arrived, he went directly to his room. He wasn't about to let his mother see this. Then she'd know no hope remained for his marrying Cora. Together they'd mucked this up very well.

He cleaned the wound with the soap and water he kept on the bureau. Removing the blood helped. Now the hole didn't look as bad as he first thought. Cora could have done him much greater damage if she'd wanted. He wrapped a clean handkerchief around his hand which would do until he could get Jenkins to bandage it properly.

Harry took the decanter from the tray on the bureau and poured himself three fingers of brandy. At this rate, he's become a drunkard. Cora was definitely not bringing out the best in him. As a matter of fact, the worst in him was needed to do what must to be done. Cora would have no choice but to marry him, after he was through.

He downed his drink in two gulps and

poured himself another. There wasn't enough whiskey or brandy in the world to fortify him for what he had to do. But do the deed he must. He threw his glass against the back wall of the fireplace, sending sparkling shards into the fire. He had no choice.

*****

After dinner, Cora sat on the blue brocade settee with Asa. He had his arm around her shoulders and from where she rested her head she heard his heart beating strong in his chest.

"Tell me about the war. What was it like?"

She felt him shrug.

"It was war and it was terrible."

"Would you rather not talk about it?"

He was quiet for a moment.

She waited, knowing this was important and not wanting to push him.

"I was with men who didn't know if they were shooting at their brothers because they had joined the Confederacy. Can you imagine? What if you found out your brother died at a battle where you fought, too? If it were me, I'd wonder for the rest of my days if my bullet was the one that killed him. The war was a great tragedy for this country. Maybe the biggest one ever and I hope it is the worst we ever do to ourselves."

"How were you wounded?"

"I was at the battle of Appomattox Courthouse. The sounds of the war raged around me. We were ordered to advance and the Confederates brought out their cannons, just as we did ours. One of the cannon balls hit me in the leg, shattering my ankle and foot. I was lucky. The doctors could save my leg from just below my knee, a lot of men lost the leg up to the hip or even lost both legs. All things considered I was charmed."

"But you didn't see it that way, did you?" She rubbed his chest, working her fingers between the buttons and feeling his warm skin against hers. Easing him as much as she could and still be circumspect.

He squeezed her shoulders. "No. I didn't think I was lucky until I came back and found you hadn't married yet. That maybe I still had a chance to make you my wife."

She moved her arm down to his waist and held it there. "I grieved for you and for Virgil for years. Only in the past year did I find the strength I needed to move on. I wanted a husband and a family. A great many men were lost during the war, making it harder to find a husband. Perhaps it was my grief, or my independent streak, but I couldn't find a husband in New York, so I became a mail-order bride."

"I'm sorry, Cora, for putting you though that. I wouldn't blame you if you sent me on my way like you did Harry. There're lots of men in San Francisco. Single men looking for a wife. You could have your pick."

"I've discovered that I don't want just any man. I want a man I know. One who is my friend as well as my husband. I want us to be able to talk about anything and everything. But I have to know that I can trust him, that he'll be around when things get hard."

"I'll be that man for you, Cora." He cupped his hand around her shoulder. "You can trust me. I've learned my lesson and I still got lucky because you are here and so am I."

He lifted her head with his knuckle. "I'm so fortunate you weren't married. So damn blessed."

Asa slanted his mouth over hers. She didn't wait for him, but pushed against his lips with her tongue. He opened, tasting of coffee and molasses cookies. Cora loved the taste of him, that something she couldn't identify. His unique flavor. She raised her arms and wrapped them around his neck, bringing her close, bosom to chest. Her nipples hardened and she felt an ache such as she'd never known deep inside.

She tugged away her lips to catch her breath.

"Cora." Asa demanded her lips, hauling her tightly against him.

The kiss was heady and fierce. Their lips joined and parted and joined again.

Slowly he ended the kiss, his breathing labored. "Send me home, Cora. I want you too much to be responsible, if you don't send me away now."

"I enjoy your kisses," she caressed his cheek. "But I think you *do* need to go, before your lips seduce me and I forget who I am."

He rested his forehead against hers. "You're a smart woman, Cora. But that's not what you should say to a man who wants you as much as I do. Just tell me to leave."

"Leave," she whispered against his lips.

They unwound from each other and Asa stood, followed by Cora. He walked across the room, took his wide-brimmed hat from the peg on the wall before heading out the door.

Cora followed him downstairs.

"Until tomorrow, sweet Cora." He raised her hand to his lips and kissed the inside of her wrist.

At the tickle on her skin, she sucked in a breath and was rewarded with a smile. "Tomorrow," she repeated as she shut and locked the door behind him.

Once she got upstairs to her little apartment, she undressed for bed. As she slid the flannel gown over her head she wondered what would have happened if she didn't send Asa home. One side of her wanted very much to make love with him. That was the same side that still had her in the grips of lust, all her feelings concentrated in her groin.

The other part of her was an unmarried woman who wondered if he would still care for her if she gave in to her desires. This was the side she listened to, though sometimes she wished she didn't.

CHAPTER 9

A week after the incident with Harry, Nellie came by Creations by Cora for her fitting. The emerald silk with roses embroidered on the hem in silver thread was as gorgeous as Cora had hoped it would be. Nellie's figure showed off the dress to perfection, though Nellie argued it was the dress that showed off her figure.

Blake came with Nellie and sat in the show room waiting for her to come and show him the dress. She parted the curtains and entered. Blake sprang to his feet.

"Well done, Cora. Nellie you look spectacular." He took her hand and twirled her as though they were dancing. "All of the women at the party on Saturday will be green with envy, and not one of them will look as beautiful as you do."

Nellie smiled. "Every one of them will want to know where I got this lovely creation. In no time you'll have more work than you can handle."

Cora replaced a pin on the cushion she had tied to her wrist. "From your lips to God's ears. I'm just so happy you like it."

"Like it? I love it." She twirled again in front of the mirrors watching how the material of the skirt flowed from the waist and seemed to float when she moved.

"Oh, Cora. Your design is so beautiful. It's like you had me in mind when you designed it."

"I did." Cora laughed. "I knew it was perfect for you."

Blake sat again and watched Nellie test the dress, sitting, standing, twirling. "What are you going to do when all my associate's wives come and want new dresses done? You'll have to hire someone. Maybe several someones."

"I'll cross that bridge when I come to it. I'm just thrilled that you're happy."

"I love how you built the corset right into the dress. That's totally new and different."

"It will make the gown much more

comfortable to wear. Of course, the fittings are that much more important in order to get the fit just right."

Nellie stopped and looked at Cora in the mirror, tilting her head. "But you only fitted me once."

"I already knew your measurements from our journey here and by altering the dresses you had with you then. I understand that getting you the dresses in time was a rushed job, but the seamstress who did the work didn't do the job very well. We had to fix every garment you packed."

"That's true. *You* fixed every one. All I did was stand still while you pinned me."

"Well, however you did it, the dress turned out wonderful." Blake cocked his head and watched his wife, smiling at her delight. "Nellie looks even more beautiful than ever."

Nellie gave him a wide smile. "I'm glad you think so."

"All right let's get you out of this and I'll wrap it up for you to take home."

Nellie and Cora went through the curtains to the back. Cora heard the bell. "I'll be right there," she called to the newcomer.

"It's just me, Cora." Asa hollered after her.

Blake rose to greet him. "Asa. Good to see you. What brings you by Cora's shop or need I ask."

"I come every day just to visit. Someday I hope she becomes my wife, but in the mean time, I'll take whatever time with her I can get."

"Have a seat." Blake pointed at the chair next to him and they both sat. "Nellie is getting a new dress. Cora outdid herself with this one."

"The green one? I've watched her make it. She's very proud of that gown."

"She has every right to be. I've seen lots of dresses on lots of women, but none as beautiful as that one on Nellie. 'Emerald green to match Nellie's eyes' Cora says."

"I'm afraid I don't have any knowledge of dresses. Cora is the only one I have to compare to and as far as I'm concerned, she is beyond compare."

Blake chuckled. "You sound like a man in love."

"I don't deny it. If I could just get Cora to come around and marry me…" He let out a sigh. "But she's being stubborn. Not that she doesn't have a right to be, I did wrong by her, but I'm hoping she'll forgive me sometime soon."

Blake sat back in the chair and crossed his legs in front of him. "Hang in there. She'll realize what a good man you are soon enough."

Asa shook his head. "Until she forgives me and marries me, it will never be soon enough."

*****

The morning sun ascended in the sky and shone brightly on the still-sleeping city. He wished it wouldn't be out in the open but this was the easiest way. And easier was definitely better, so he'd have to make do.

He took the large bouquet of roses from the seat across from him and descended to the street. Then he walked to the door of Creations by Cora and entered. Cora always opened her shop before everyone else.

As the bell over the door sounded, she appeared, coming through the curtains from the sewing room, dressed for the day in her favorite yellow dress. He recognized it because she'd worn it on a couple of their outings. When she saw him she stopped cold.

"Harry, why did you bring me flowers? It won't change my mind. Didn't you get enough last time you were here? Why can't you understand that I don't want to see you?"

Harry didn't answer but shoved the roses in her arms and pushed past her farther into the shop. Before she could turn around, he grabbed her and held a handkerchief saturated with ether over her mouth and nose. The roses hit the floor in a fragrant mess as she struggled against him.

He kept his face averted lest he, too, succumb to the medicine's sweet, delicate scent. The arm Harry put around her waist was like steel, not to be moved, no matter how much she struggled. In less than a minute she stopped moving and sagged in his embrace. He swung her limp body up into his arms moved through the doorway, out to his waiting carriage. He didn't bother pulling the shop door shut. It didn't matter now. Asa could look forever and never find where Harry was taking Cora.

*****

Asa arrived at Cora's shop earlier than usual. He'd stopped at the bakery on the way and had fresh bread still warm from the oven in a sack. He planned to make Cora breakfast and the sourdough bread would be wonderful toasted with butter and jam.

The door to the shop stood wide open. Was Cora airing out the place? He entered and saw the pile of roses on the floor. Roses! He hurried through the store and up the stairs to her apartment. He knocked on the door, but heard no answer. Turning the knob, he found the entrance wasn't locked.

"Cora. Cora, are you here?"

No response. Concerned she might be ill; Asa set the bread on the table and went to Cora's bedroom. Empty. Where was she? She wouldn't go off and leave everything open for anyone to just wander in.

Heart pounding in his chest, he knew the answer. Someone had taken her and he knew it was Harry Belcher. Cora had said Harry wouldn't take no for an answer.

Asa didn't know the city and wasn't sure where to start looking, but he knew someone who did. He hailed a cab and gave the driver Blake Malone's address on Russian Hill.

He arrived in good time and limped quickly up the walk, his wooden leg forcing him to go slow when all he wanted was to run. At this point in time he hated the thing attached below his knee and the fact the wooden limb made him slow. If he was to save Cora, he must be quick.

Asa pounded on the front entrance.

The door opened on James. "Mr. Woods, how may I be of service?"

"I need to see Blake Malone. Right away. It's an emergency."

"Certainly, sir. Mr. and Mrs. Malone are in the dining room enjoying breakfast. If you'll follow me, please."

Asa followed as fast as he could behind the butler.

James entered the dining room through a set of dark wood, double doors. "Mr. Woods to see you, sir." He stood to one side and let Asa pass.

"Blake, Nellie. I'm sorry to interrupt your meal but I need your help right away. We have no time to waste."

Blake stood and walked to Asa. "Come, sit, have some coffee and tell us what has happened."

Asa sat but he couldn't stay still. In seconds he was up again and pacing. "He took her. Cora she's gone. He took her."

"Who took her?" Nellie's hand went to her throat and her eyes widened. "Who took

Cora?"

"Harry Belcher, that's who."

She shook her head. "No. He's the one she didn't want to see again. She wouldn't have changed her mind and gone out with him. Would she?" Nellie picked up her coffee cup and took a sip.

"No. You don't understand." Asa slammed his fist on the table.

Nellie jumped. Her cup clattered onto the saucer.

Asa took a deep breath. "I'm sorry to frighten you but Cora told him she didn't want to see him anymore. He and his mother made threats against Cora if she didn't marry him. She refused. So you see, she wouldn't have changed her mind and certainly wouldn't have left her shop door wide open. There was a bunch of roses on the floor of the shop. I think that's how he got close to Cora. She always believes the best in people. And she was certain that it was Henrietta that posed the threat to her, not Harry."

Blake sat again at the table. "This verifies what Cora told us, so I have to agree. Asa, get a cup of coffee and sit down. If we're to get Cora back we have to think about this logically."

Though he was bursting with unspent energy, Asa knew Blake was right. He needed a clear head to focus on Cora.

James brought him a cup full of hot, steaming coffee.

"Thank you, James." Asa looked around at Blake and Nellie. "Please, both of you, forgive my outburst. I'm so anxious about Cora, I don't remember my manners."

Blake waved his hand. "It's nothing. We know Harry has a home but he probably wouldn't take her there, too many people."

"He's president of a bank." Asa took a sip of coffee.

"No," Blake shook his head. "He wouldn't take her there. Again, too many people and too easy to be seen."

Nellie pushed her almost-full breakfast plate out of the way.

"I'm sorry to put you off your breakfast." Asa said. "I simply didn't know who else to talk to. I don't know anyone here in San Francisco but you and Blake."

"Nonsense. You were right to come to us." Nellie turned to Blake. "Wouldn't the city assessor be able to tell you what property Harry or his mother owns?"

"You're brilliant." Blake leaned over and kissed his wife. "What is his mother's name?"

"Henrietta," replied Asa.

Blake threw his napkin down as he stood. "James, have the coach brought around quick."

The butler nodded and quickly removed himself from his station by the buffet to get the carriage.

"I'll stay here in case Cora does manage to get away." Nellie's voice broke and her eyes filled with tears. "Just in case."

Blake took his wife in his arms. "We'll get her back. Don't worry."

Nellie nodded and wiped away her tears with the back of her hand. "I'm not worried. I have complete faith in you."

Blake nodded and kissed her lightly on the lips before turning back to Asa. "Come with me Asa. They can't have that many properties. I'd never heard of them until you and Cora came here. I know the majority of the extremely wealthy families."

Asa squeezed and released his fists again and again as he walked next to Blake toward the front door of the house. All he wanted was to hurry and go after Cora, but he must remain polite if he wanted help. "Do you know all the wealthy people in the city?"

"No. But I know the powerful ones. They're the people who help with my business adventures."

Asa cocked his eyebrow. "Adventures?"

"That's what it feels like sometimes when I start a new business…at least with this newest one. I'm thinking of calling it an amusement park. There will be all kinds of things from a picnic area to water boats and shooting galleries. Every form of entertainments for families that I can provide will be there…eventually."

"I like the idea."

"Good. Ah, here's our transportation."

The carriage pulled to a stop in front of the house. Blake gave instructions to his driver, then he and Asa climbed in.

"So, tell me Asa, once we get Cora back, and I have no doubt that we will, are you planning on marrying her?"

"I would in a minute if she'd just say yes. I'm afraid I really mucked things up. I should have come home and let her decide about my leg."

Blake cocked an eyebrow and nodded. "You were afraid she would reject you.

That's an understandable reaction."

Asa bounced his good leg then crossed his knee and uncrossed it and crossed it again. He rubbed his thigh. Even though he'd lost his leg below the knee, he still had phantom pain and rubbing his thigh sometimes helped. "Yes, and now I know better. Cora is a strong woman and she's wouldn't have let something like a missing leg stop her from marrying me. But now she's not sure she can trust me. I have to rebuild the relationship we had before I went to war."

Blake nodded. "Nellie and I haven't been married but a few months. Building a rapport is difficult."

"At least Nellie married you and is giving you the chance." *Cora hasn't agreed to marry me, but when we find her, I'm not letting her out of my sight again.* "When we find her, she'll either marry me or...I don't know what but I'll sleep in her sewing room if need be."

Blake chuckled. "You've got it bad."

"Got what bad?"

"Love. Nellie and I had to work through problems, too. But we did and now we're in love and expecting a baby."

"You are lucky." Asa sighed. "I hope Cora will come around. I know that love is part and parcel of a happy marriage. I watched my parents together for nearly thirty years. They loved each other very much and that's what I want with Cora."

"I hope you get it."

The carriage slowed and then stopped.

"We're here. Let's go see what kinds of property the Belchers own. Then we'll split up and check them out. If I need to I'll get my partner, Nick Cartwright, to help us."

"I appreciate all you're doing."

Blake nodded. "I'm helping a friend and you're welcome. Now let's see what we've got to work with."

In the City Assessor's office they discovered Harry didn't own any property. The house and two warehouses were owned by his mother.

Blake donned his hat and gloves. "He won't take her back to the house we know that. One of the warehouses is our best bet. Do you have a gun?"

Asa shook his head. "No. I haven't carried one since the war."

"You'll need one now. Here take mine. I'll get my driver's. The warehouses are in the same area. I'll drop you off at the first one and drive on to the second."

Asa nodded, his throat too tight to speak. *What if they were too late? What if Harry decided to kill her rather than let her marry someone else?* Asa didn't really believe that. He thought he knew what Harry had in mind. After the threat by Harry's mother, Asa knew that marrying Cora was paramount to them for some reason. No, Harry planned to rape Cora so she'd think she had no option but to marry him.

*****

Cora sat across from Harry in the carriage, her ankles and wrists tied. The rope cut into her wrists and blood coated her bonds. *How dare he kidnap her! I never thought Harry would do something like this.*

"Where are you taking me?"

He sat straight in the seat and kept looking out the window, probably checking the road behind them. This was not the easy going Harry she knew.

Frowning, he said, "What does it matter? There's nothing you can do about the situation anyway so I'll tell you. Mother has a warehouse down by the wharf. It's empty at this time, waiting for the ships to come in with their silks, spices and other riches. The ship owners rent the building just a few months at a time, so they don't have the expense of owning a building that is empty for half the year. Of course, it also comes in handy when a circumstance like this one appear."

"Are you going to kill me Harry? Make sure I can't marry Asa or anyone else?"

"No, my dear." He shook his head. "I wish it was that simple."

Bile rose from her stomach. If he didn't plan to kill her, what would he do?

"You don't have to do this Harry. We can work something out."

"I don't think so. You've been given ample opportunity to marry me but have refused. I'm ensuring you don't have any other option."

Blood pounded in her ears. She knew now what he had planned. Harry was going to spoil her for any other man. Her hands shook and started to sweat. She'd rather he just kill her.

"I won't let you take me. You'll have to kill me, Harry."

"Tsk, tsk. Make it easy on yourself, Cora."

"I'll fight you with every breath in my body."

"Actually, I hope you do. I like it when they fight. My previous wives always fought me, but in the end it doesn't matter. I'll get what I want whether you're conscious or not. Up to you."

Cora's eyes widened at the same time her stomach knotted. "You killed them didn't you?"

"Unfortunately, they couldn't give me children, so Mother had them disposed of."

She swallowed hard. "Disposed of?"

"Will you repeat everything I say?"

Even in the dim illumination of the carriage lamps she saw anger light in his eyes for just an instant.

"Um, no. You're insane, you know."

She immediately regretted the words. He acted like she'd just insulted him, which she guessed she had.

He turned to her, wild-eyed. "I'm not. I didn't get rid of those women. Mother did. She's the insane one."

Don't make him mad. Keep him calm.

"Of course." She needed to keep him talking. "How many women has she gotten rid of?"

"Just four. Three of them I was married to." He picked some lint from his sleeve. The fourth was a poor Chinese girl. It's too bad though. I really liked all of them, but Mother insists on there being a child. Me, I don't really care about a kid, but I do care about the money she'll leave the little brat. I want that money and won't get it if there is not a child. Don't you understand?"

Whether she kept him calm or not, she couldn't stop the words from flowing. "I understand perfectly." Under her breath she added, "you *and* your mother are insane."

Four! She's killed four women! And I'll be number five because I won't let him do what he wants. I won't.

Harry ignored her outburst. "Mother was to wait for us at the warehouse. She wanted to make sure the deed is done and there is no turning back for you. But I convinced her I wouldn't be able to perform with her there. So you see, Cora, I'm sparing you where I can, but you won't have any choice. Not if you want to live."

"If those are my only choices, live with you after you rape me or die, I'd rather die."

Harry reached over the expanse between them and slapped her across the face. "There will be no more talk like that." He sat back, stretched his legs and crossed them at the ankles. "If I have to Cora, I'll keep you tied up except for when I use you. Now, you don't want to live like that, do you?"

Cora shook her head, her face stinging and the coppery taste of blood filled her mouth from where her teeth had dug into her cheek. If she opened her mouth and said what she thought she'd only be struck again. She was smarter than that.

The carriage stopped. Harry pulled Cora to her feet by her wrists and made her stand in the doorway while he stepped down to the ground. Then he slung her over his shoulder like she was a side of beef. He was stronger than he appeared, carrying Cora like she weighed nothing.

His driver got out and held the door to the warehouse open for Harry. It appeared to Cora, the man had done this before. He was a big man with dirty matted hair under his top hat. He smiled at her revealing black, rotting teeth. Taking a good look at him now, Cora decided he was probably the one who'd 'gotten rid' of the other wives. A stench hung about him that had nothing to do with the way he smelled.

Harry walked across the empty warehouse, his boots and those of his driver tapping a rapid tattoo on the wooden floor. At the bottom of a set of stairs, Harry adjusted Cora so she was tight across his shoulder and climbed the stairs to the room above.

She didn't know exactly how big the warehouse was, but it appeared to be huge. Even if Asa found them, he'd have to go through the driver before he ever reached Cora.

At the top of the stairs was an office. The room was unlike any office she'd ever been in and obviously had been used before, presumably by Harry, for such activity as he planned for Cora. Normal office furniture, a desk, chair, file cabinets were present but where there might have been a settee or a couple of chairs, there was a bed.

Harry threw her down on the mattress and she bounced a couple of times.

"I'm cutting the ropes around your ankles, so be still and don't make me regret the gesture. My driver is outside and will shoot you, if need be. The man has no conscience. Don't run. If you do, not only I will take you anyway, but I'll let him have you, too. So you see, he's hoping you do run. Do we understand each other?"

"Yes. I understand. You sick bastard." She understood all right. Resoluteness in his expression told her he would do this. Nothing she could say would change his mind. She wouldn't try to run, she didn't want to have to deal with the driver but she would fight to the best of her ability.

"Names, dear." Sneering, he backhanded her across the face. "I don't like being called names. You will refrain from doing so."

Cora rubbed the back of her tied hands across her mouth and then looked at the result. Blood smeared her hand and the coppery taste of the red fluid filled her mouth again.

"Now see what you made me do." He took the kerchief from his pocket and dabbed at her lip. "Your poor lip, but it will heal. Just don't make me punish you again."

"You've had three wives and one poor Chinese girl, none of whom got pregnant. Have you ever considered the problem may be yours?"

His eyes shot wide, and he backhanded her again. "It's not me. I've just chosen the wrong women. You'll see. You'll be the one."

Cora was sure now she saw the light of insanity in his eyes. It wasn't a trick of the lamp light in the carriage. How could she not have seen it before? Had she wanted to just see the gentleman who courted her? What about those encounters with Asa? She realized she'd seen it then. The tightly controlled temper, the errors in judgment and the anger he'd shown toward his mother's threats against Cora. She thought it had been on her behalf, but was it?

"Now, my dear, we must get you out of those clothes. I can't make you mine with you dressed."

He pulled her up by the rope at her wrists.

The pain she felt, was nothing compared to what was coming. Once she had a firm stance, she snatched her wrists from his hand and slammed them up against his jaw.

Harry's head snapped to the right with her blow, but it didn't knock him down as she'd hoped.

"Want to do this the hard way, do you? Fine." He grabbed the front of her dress at the neck and pulled, shredding the material down to her waist. With his knife he sliced apart the hooks on the front of her corset, revealing her chemise. Then he gripped the front of that garment and rendered it apart, baring her skin.

Her blood roared in her veins, and her stomach knotted, but she wouldn't show her fear.

"You're quite lovely, my dear. I knew you would be. Your breasts with their pale pink nipples saved just for me." He dropped the knife, grasped a breast in each hand and squeezed hard.

"Ow. That hurts." Pain throbbed in her tender tissue. She tried to pull away but he simply squeezed harder, holding her fast.

"Of course it does. That's how you like it. You *all* like the pain, so I give it to you." He pushed her down to the bed again. "I'll give you all the pain you want."

A commotion of shouts and scuffling sounded from outside in the warehouse. A shot rang out, and then someone with an awkward gait pounded up the stairs.

Asa!

The door to the office burst open and Asa stood there in his dark fury, aiming a pistol at Harry.

Harry had made the mistake of leaving

her legs unbound and hanging off the bed. She kicked up with her right leg and her knee caught him in the groin.

Emitting a shout, he fell back from her and then to his knees.

Asa came forward and knocked Harry, who was moaning and holding himself, over onto his side.

Asa looked at her and smiled. "Remind me not to make you mad." He unknotted the ropes and freed her wrists then took off his coat and wrapped it around her shoulders. "Are you all right?"

Cora put her arms in the sleeves and pulled the coat tightly around herself, then nodded and stared at the floor. *All right? Nothing is all right*

Asa put a knuckle under her chin and raised her head so she'd look at him but she turned away.

"Cora? Did he hurt you?"

She shook her head. "No. I'm fine."

Asa gave her a small smile. "You're not fine, but you will be. Together we'll both be all right."

She turned her head away so he couldn't see the tears roll down her cheeks. She would not cry. *She would not cry.* Harry wasn't getting the satisfaction of knowing how much he'd hurt her. Her insides churned, bile rose and burned her throat, but he would never know. Nor would Asa. This was her problem, not his.

Asa took the ropes that had bound Cora's wrists and hog-tied Harry. He wasn't going anywhere until the police took him away.

Cora stood, and then walked to where Harry lay helpless on the floor, his wrists tied to his ankles. She wanted to kick him, but refrained, instead she hoped the position was as painful as it looked.

"You'll never hurt anyone again Harry. If you're smart and don't want to be charged with the murder of your three previous wives and that Chinese girl, you'll tell the police about your mother. I'm telling them everything I know."

Harry looked upward, anger narrowing his eyes. "You should have just married me and none of this would have happened."

"And have you murder me when I can't give you children either? Because it's *you* who has the problem not your wives. *You* are the one who can't have children. Even if you don't die in prison, you will never give your mother a grandchild. I hope the families of those murdered young women come forward and take everything you and your mother own. You won't need it while you spend your life in prison, assuming they don't hang you instead."

"Hang me!" Real panic marred his handsome features. "But I didn't kill anyone. Mother did."

"You better make sure the police, and a jury, believe you."

Asa took her by the elbow and led her from the room. When they got to the bottom of the stairs, he put his arm around her shoulders. "Don't look, Cora."

She spotted the body of the driver before Asa had her look away. He'd been shot one time through the head.

Gagging, Cora turned quickly away. "Asa, did you do that?"

"Yes." His voice was low and emotionless.

"You're a very good shot."

"I was a sniper in the war. My life depended on being accurate the first time."

"And now, so did mine."

He squeezed her shoulders. "We'll get through this together, Cora. Trust me."

"There is nothing to 'get through'. It's over." She took a deep breath. "I'm safe and Harry and his mother are going away for their lifetimes."

"You're right. Let's go home."

They exited the warehouse at the same time Blake's coach pulled up.

"You found her." Blake jumped from the carriage almost before it came to a full stop.

"Yes. She's unhurt and Harry is trussed up like a pig waiting for the police to come. And there's a body. I was forced to shoot Harry's driver."

Blake nodded. "I'll stay here, you get Cora home. Otis will take you to the police on the way. There's a station not far from here where Cora can give her statement."

"Thank you, but how will you get home?" Cora asked.

"Otis will come back for me after he drops you two off at Cora's place."

"Let's get you home." Asa looked at her. "I'll even help you heat the water for a hot bath. You'll feel better after that."

Asa looked at her.

Wincing, she swore she saw pity in his eyes.

She didn't want his, or anyone else's, pity. "I'll be fine on my own. You don't have to stay."

He furrowed his brows and sighed. "You've been through a horrific experience. I don't think you should be alone."

"Don't you understand? I don't want you or anyone else there with me. I don't want your pity. I want to be alone!" she shouted at Asa, one of the few people who had been nothing but kind to her. She burst into tears. "I'm sorry. I'm sorry."

Asa wrapped his arms around her and swayed. "It's all right, sweetheart. It's all right."

She stood in his arms, crying, and wondered if anything would be all right again.

CHAPTER 10

Once they got in the carriage, Asa kept his arm around her shoulders and she appreciated his warmth. The cold she felt reached deep inside her all the way to her bones. His jacket did nothing to stop the internal chill.

They didn't speak the entire trip to the police department where she gave her statement. Nor after when he took her home. Right now Cora had nothing she wanted to talk about. Maybe someday. Maybe with Nellie, but not with Asa.

Moving slowly, he helped her up the stairs and into her bedroom.

"I'll leave you to take off your dress in

private. Get into your night clothes while I start heating the water for your bath."

Cora nodded and watched him leave the room. Then she took off his jacket and let the rest of her clothes fall to the floor. Bruises already darkened her breasts where Harry had squeezed them. Her wrists were bloody. She went to the bureau and poured water from the pitcher into the adjacent basin. Then she washed off the smears of blood. The soap stung, but after she was done she saw the damage the ropes had wrought.

Wide abrasions marked both wrists. She patted her skin dry but the blood still seeped. She needed Asa to bandage her.

Her night rail and dressing gown were on the foot of her bed. She quickly donned them and wiped the blood away.

When she entered the kitchen, she saw Asa pouring hot water into two cups and a metal bucket on the stove full of water, presumably for her bath.

She didn't want a bath. She just wanted to go to bed. Maybe when she awoke, this would all be nothing more than a horrible nightmare.

He looked up at her approach. "There

you are. The tea should be ready in a few minutes."

"Thank you. I need your help to bandage my wrists." She held them up so he could see the wounds.

Asa squeezed shut his eyes. "The bastard. I should have killed him instead of just tying him up."

She found his anger on her behalf comforting and placed her hand on his chest. "You're not a murderer. Bandage me and then we'll have tea and you can go back to the hotel. I've already caused you enough trouble for one evening."

Slowly, with infinite care, he brought the back of his fingers down her cheek. "I'm not going anywhere. You don't need to be alone tonight."

She shook her head. "You can't stay here. What would people think?"

"No one who matters will think a thing about it. But if you don't want me to stay then I'll take you to Blake and Nellie's. Either way, you won't be by yourself."

With a sigh, she nodded. "All right you can stay, but only because I don't want to be a burden on Nellie and Blake. They've already done so much for me."

"*You* are never a burden."

"Thank you." She backed away and the loss of his warmth sped through her causing shivers to run up and down her spine. She wondered if she'd ever feel warm again.

"You're freezing. After I wrap your wrists, we'll sit on the settee, and I'll hold you."

She nodded afraid to speak. Afraid to ask for what she needed. Finally, she said, "That would be nice." *Nice!* She craved the warmth he provided. He was her safe haven. But Asa seemed to know that. "You'll find cloth and some salve in the cupboard above the sink."

Asa retrieved the items and bandaged her wrists. "There does that feel better?"

"Yes. It actually does."

"Come now." He took her hand and led her to the sofa. "Sit with me."

She followed. Her whole body felt heavy, her energy gone, drained as though she'd run for miles. "What about the tea?"

"I'll get that in a few minutes. For the time being, I need you in my arms."

They settled on the couch where she rested her head on his chest and her arm on his waist, getting closer to ease the cold from her body.

"Do you want to talk about it?"

She shook her head. "No. Just hold me. Don't let me go, Asa."

"I won't. Not ever."

He kissed her forehead and then pressed his lips against hers in a whisper-soft kiss that only gave and didn't take.

"Thank you for coming for me," she said the words so quietly, she thought he didn't hear.

"I will always come for you, Cora." He squeezed her to him and stroked a hand over her hair. "Always."

She settled back against him. His mere presence soothed her. The thump of his heart beating in his chest comforted her. She didn't want to leave his embrace. Barely able to keep her eyes open, she finally gave in and closed them.

When she awoke, she was still in Asa's arms...and she was also in bed. He hadn't let her go all night but had remained a gentleman, too. She was never afraid he wouldn't. Asa loved her. She knew that and something besides gratitude lived in her heart for the man. A soft, warm feeling enveloped her, had always been with her, whenever she thought of Asa. Was that love? Was love the soft glow she felt or was love the overwhelming longing to be with someone? Could it be both?

She should be outraged that he slept in her bed with her, but they were both dressed. He had taken off his pants, boots and the wooden leg. But he kept on his long johns.

"Does it bother you?" His chest rumbled with his words.

"No, I'm curious is all. Does it hurt?"

"Not really. My leg is uncomfortable by the end of the day which is why I took the wooden one off last night." He turned, tucked her closer against him. "I get what they call phantom pain where it feels like my leg is still there and hurting, but rubbing my thigh, usually helps the feeling go away."

"Why is that do you suppose?"

"I guess because everything's connected or at least it used to be."

Stretching out her arms, she yawned. "Um...we really should get up."

"Uh, uh, I'd have to let you go then, and I don't want to ever let you go."

"Asa," she turned in his arms and placed a hand on his chest. "We have to get up. I have a business to run. I can't stay in bed all day."

"Would you, if you could?"

She heard the hopeful note. Would she? The way she was feeling it was a definite possibility.

"I don't know," she answered honestly. "I don't know anything right now, except I want my life back to normal. I don't want to think about what happened to me. Ever."

"You'll have to testify at his trial and maybe that of his mother as well."

"I know. I don't like the idea. I don't want to ever see them again. But I'll testify so they both go to prison for a long time."

"That won't be easy on you. Their attorney will say it was your fault—alienation of affection."

Her eyes narrowed, outrage flowing through her like fire, making her ready to boil over. "I didn't lead him on."

Asa put up his hands in surrender. "I know that, but you did come out here to marry him and then didn't do it. Because of me."

"Thank God I didn't. Do you know he's been married three times before me? You being alive and coming here for me probably saved my life. Finding me before...before he could...could you know. You saved my life again."

She untangled herself from Asa's arms and was immediately bereft. The warmth and safety he provided were absent even though he was still in the room. She'd never felt this way before and she didn't like it. Didn't want to feel so needy.

"I must get dressed and you need to leave."

Asa sat up and put his legs over the side of the bed. He picked his wooden leg off the floor, shoved his knee into it and attached it to his thigh with metal clamps, and then he put on his pants and boots.

Interesting. Cora watched in fascination.

"Does it bother you now? Watching me get dressed?"

She shook her head. "Heavens no, other than I've never seen a man in his drawers before. But seeing you put on your leg is intriguing, that's all."

He smiled. "I should have known you would only see it as something new to understand. Your curiosity always did get you into trouble."

"When we were younger," she shook her

head, "neither you nor Virgil, understood my need to know how things worked. Now you think it's a good trait."

"Now I have that keen mind of yours directed at me and my leg. I find it's helpful to make me more comfortable. Believe it or not, other than my doctors, you are the only person to see my stump or to see me without my wooden leg."

"Then I'm honored you would trust me that much. I know it's got to be difficult."

"Very. But now that you've seen it for the first time, it will be easier for me next time. Eventually, I won't think about it and neither will you."

"You're assuming we'll marry. I'm not ready to make that promise."

"I'll wait for you as long as it takes."

"Well," she sighed and rubbed at a forming headache. She didn't want to talk about this now. "You're dressed, so please remove yourself to the kitchen while I change my clothes and clean up."

He saluted her. "Yes, ma'am. I'll start coffee."

After Asa left, Cora changed into her favorite red dress with white lace at the neck and cuffs. She fingered the ring on the chain around her neck. It was her father's wedding ring and wearing it always brought her a measure of peace, even in times like this.

Wearing this dress made her feel stronger and strength was what she needed now. The water in the basin was cool and perfect to clear the sleep from her eyes and wake up. She washed her face and hands, cleaned her teeth with tooth powder and brushed her hair. After she did so, her locks shone in the sunlight with copper highlights that accented her eyes. She gathered the heavy mass into a bun at the nape of her neck.

The clothes she'd worn yesterday were still in a pile on the floor. She didn't want to touch them but knew she had to. After gathering the dress, chemise and corset she rolled them up and took them to the kitchen.

Asa looked up from the table where he sat with a cup of coffee in front of him. "There you are. You look beautiful."

Her cheeks heated and she smiled. "Thank you. I could look a wreck and you would still tell me I'm beautiful."

"Because you are. I've made enough mistakes, I won't lie to you. You are a beautiful woman, always have been. You just don't realize it now and didn't know it before either."

With determined moves, she took the wadded up clothes, put them in the waste can, and then sat across the table from him.

"Do you want me to take that out for you?" He nodded toward the trash can.

"Can you burn them?"

"If that's what you want, that's what we'll do. I'll take them out back to burn or we can cut the material into strips and burn them here in your stove."

"No. I don't want those clothes in this room any longer than necessary. The incinerator will do." She went to the cupboard and took down the box of oatmeal and held it up. "I can't turn this into ash."

"But," Asa chuckled, "when you burn things it's so spectacular."

"It was wasn't it?" Cora shook her head and laughed.

After breakfast Asa walked to the alley and destroyed her clothes, shoving them into the iron incinerator. He didn't blame her for not wanting to try and repair them. He knew if repairs could be made, Cora was the one who could do it. But the clothes held such bad memories, she'd never be able to wear the dress again anyway.

Today he wanted to see Blake and find out what would happen to Harry and his mother. Cora had told Harry he'd spend the rest of his life in prison but Asa knew that outcome wasn't necessarily so.

Blake may not have thought they were powerful, but Harry was president of a bank, and as such had helped out many a politician or judge. Asa was sure he had favors he could call in.

Back inside he saw Cora helping a customer in the front of the shop. He watched her to be sure she was calm and could handle the transaction. He waited until she was through and back in the sewing room to talk to her.

"I'm going to see Blake. Do you want me to wait until this evening and then we can go together?"

"Oh, yes. I'd like to talk to Nellie, and to thank Blake again for all the help he gave you. How did you find me anyway?"

Asa told her about Nellie suggesting the City Assessor's office.

"I never would have thought of that. I'm so glad she did."

He looked around and out through the

open curtains into the shop before taking her by the waist and bringing her close. "You can't imagine how scared I was that I might lose you."

Shaking her head, she rested her hands on his chest. "No more afraid than I was, I assure you."

"I think you are the strongest, bravest woman I've ever known. After all that's happened to you, you still opened your shop and are working as though it's just another day."

She stiffened.

He knew then she was not as good as she pretended.

"It is just another day. I'm not letting what happened affect me. I still have a business to run and customers to..." her voice trailed off and he watched the tears fill her eyes.

Asa wrapped her in his arms. She circled her arms around his waist and laid her head against his chest and sobbed. He let her cry for as long as she needed.

She sniffled, pulled away from him, then took her hanky from her sleeve, dabbed at her eyes and blew her nose.

"Feel better?"

She nodded. "I'm sorry for that outburst."

"Don't be. You should close your shop and we can go see Nellie and Blake sooner rather than later."

Cora walked to the door, turned over the closed sign and then went upstairs to her apartment. All her limbs felt like weights were attached, so she could hardly walk up the stairs. Her eyes might as well have been filled with sand, they ached so much from crying.

When she reached her bedroom, she glanced at herself in the mirror above the bureau. Seeing her red, swollen eyes staring back, she rinsed a wash cloth in the water from the pitcher and held the cool, soothing cloth over her sore eyes.

Asa followed her and silently watched.

When she was done, she turned to where he leaned against the door jamb.

"Now are you feeling better?" He stood upright and walked to her.

"Yes, I am. I guess I needed to get emotion out of my system."

He nodded. "I would imagine. You went through a terrible experience. You might need to cry a lot more in the coming days, and it's all right if you do."

"I'm fine. I need to talk to Nellie, that's all. She'll understand. She'll know what to do."

Asa didn't say anything but waited for Cora to get her wrap and come with him to catch a cab to the Malone's. His fear grew every time Cora said she was fine. He knew she wasn't but he also knew she had to come to that realization herself, just as he'd done when he was wounded. A solution was not easily found but together they could get through this and he could help her, if she let him.

CHAPTER 11

They arrived at Blake and Nellie's in short order and walked up the long cobblestone path to the front door, where Asa knocked.

James opened the door, ever his tidy self, in his black suit and white shirt, tie and gloves.

"Mr. Woods, Miss Jones, please come in. If you'll wait here, I'll tell Mr. Malone you are here."

"No need, James." Asa watched as Nellie descended the stairs. Floated was more like it in her blue silk dress. Except for Cora, he'd never seen anyone as graceful. She held the front of the skirt with her hands so she wouldn't trip. The action also happened to give onlookers from the bottom of the stairs a glimpse of shapely ankle and matching blue silk shoes.

When she got to the bottom of the stairs, she took Cora in her arms and gave her a hug.

"I'm so glad you've come. Please follow me to the library. I'm sure that's where Blake has holed up. Probably working on plans for the family emporium he and Nick are building."

Asa nodded. "He talked a little about that yesterday. It sounds like quite an ambitious venture."

"Oh, it is but I think it will be wonderful." Nellie hooked her arm through Cora's as they walked. "A place where families can go have fun is needed. San Francisco is growing and we have to take care of our families too, not just the men."

"You sound as enthusiastic as your husband." Asa walked behind the two women. He was glad Cora had agreed to come along. Nellie was the one person he knew Cora could talk to, now if she just would.

Blake sat behind a large, mahogany desk, bent over what Asa thought were plans. He looked up when he heard them enter and then came over to them. He gave

Nellie a kiss on the cheek to which she blushed profusely and Blake chuckled.

"She always blushes so prettily when I kiss her. I wonder if she still will when she gets used to me."

Nellie swatted him lightly. "Blake stop, you're embarrassing me."

"Sorry, my dear. I shouldn't tease you." He turned to Asa and Cora. "To what do we owe the pleasure of your company today?"

Cora went from Nellie's arm to Asa's and hung on tightly as though he was her anchor in a storm.

"I wanted to thank you for coming with Asa and finding me. I don't know what...what would..." She began to cry.

Asa squeezed her tightly. "She's a bit overwhelmed."

"Cora? Honey?" Nellie placed her hand on Cora's shoulder. "Why don't you come with me?"

Cora nodded and then, wrapped her arms around Nellie's waist and sobbed into the taller woman's chest.

"Shh, it'll be all right. Let's go have some tea in the parlor.

As they watched the women walk away, Blake clapped Asa on the back. "She'll be okay. Nellie will take care of her."

"I know. Nellie is her dearest friend," Asa then turned to Blake. "Cora told me some about their trip over here. They became very close."

Blake nodded. "To bad you didn't get to meet Annie. She's their friend, too, but William, her new husband, lives on the far side of the city. Visiting will be difficult. Nellie found it very upsetting when he whisked Annie away after the ceremony without giving the women time for a proper goodbye."

"I suppose he was just in a hurry to get home. You know how new husbands are."

"I suppose so," Blake chuckled.

*****

Nellie poured a cup of tea for Cora and handed it to her. "There you go. Drink a little. I find a cup of tea helps in every situation. It's comforting."

Cora nodded and with a shaky hand, took the tea. "It is. Thank you for helping to find me. Asa told me you what you did. They wouldn't have find out what property Harry and his mother owned without your suggestion. They wouldn't have found me if not for you."

Great, fat tears rolled down her cheeks and Cora was unable to keep them at bay, no matter how much she wanted to. Nellie wouldn't mind the tears, but Cora did. She didn't want to cry. She wanted to be strong, but...she couldn't.

"Here now, you cry all you want." Nellie gave her a fresh handkerchief. "You're safe and Harry is behind bars. Blake told me they picked up his mother in a carriage just outside the warehouse. She was waiting to make sure the deed had been done."

"I'm glad they got her," Cora said fiercely. "I hope she hangs for what she did to those other women." She sounded a bit bloodthirsty, but Henrietta brought so much grief to so many people with her insane machinations.

"Oh yes, his other wives."

Cora nodded and blew her nose. "Yes. I can't call them wives, they were brought here to be breeding stock so Henrietta could get grandchildren to leave her wealth to. That's why I was brought here, too."

"Why wouldn't she just leave it to Harry?"

"I think she was afraid he'd lose it

gambling, so she wanted to leave it to her grandchild. She was just an insane old woman, with strange ideas."

"I know, Blake told me. Isn't it awful?"

"It is, but now she won't be able to hurt another woman ever again." Cora closed her aching eyes for a moment. "I'm an idiot. I should never have considered marrying Harry after Asa arrived. When I think back on it, I believe I wanted to punish Asa for what he did to me…making me grieve for him. I missed him, Nellie. More than I ever thought I could. We were friends, but it was more for me, because it hurt so much when he died." She shook her head. "I mean when I thought he was dead. And now, he's been nothing but kind to me. How do I repay him for all he's done for me? So far all I've done is keep him at bay and yell at him when he tries to help me."

"I don't know. It's a difficult situation you're in. But I think you already know what to do. You love Asa, even if you won't admit it now, you will soon."

Cora shook her head. "I can't marry him. What if I do and it's not because I love him but just because he saved my life? That wouldn't be fair to Asa."

Nellie let out a long sigh. "I know you love him and you do too, but you've just escaped having a terrible, heinous act performed against you. You can't just overcome that fear, literally overnight. Give yourself some time. Don't rush into anything right now."

Cora knew Nellie was right. She needed to let her feelings settle and learn for herself what she felt for Asa. Was it love? Was that really why it hurt so much when she thought he died? Was she just afraid of being alone? With Virgil and Asa both gone she'd had no choice. There was literally no one to care for her but herself. During those years, she'd become very independent. Was she willing to give up that independence to marry Asa? Did she love him enough to put herself second?

Cora didn't know. With every answer came another question. The biggest one— did she love Asa? Love would trump everything else and that was why she had to be sure.

But how do you really know if you love someone? What was love? Was love the fact that she missed Asa when he wasn't there? Or that she was filled with joy whenever he walked through the door? Was love the feeling of quiet contentment she felt when they were together, even when they were simply sitting on the sofa watching the fire?

Suddenly, her heart lifted and she knew without a doubt, love was all of those things and more. It was her heart beating a little faster every time she saw him looking at her, a quiet smile on his face. She wanted to see those smiles. Every day…for the rest of her life. She loved Asa. All the uncertainty was gone. With every last fiber of her being, she loved him.

"You've gotten awfully quiet. What are you smiling about?"

Cora turned her body so she faced Nellie. "I love him. Nellie, I love Asa. I think I always have."

"I know." Nellie smiled. "You wouldn't be this upset if you didn't love him. You could let him go. But as soon as you saw him in the hotel lobby, you knew, you just didn't know how to handle it and so you denied the feelings."

"How do you know these things?"

The smile on Nellie's face faltered a bit but she answered. "I know now that I didn't love my first husband. I mourned him because I had to, my in-laws forced me. Given the choice, I'd have worn bright green, red and purple when he died anything but black. I was relieved he didn't return. All the pain he put me through, the bruises from the beatings he gave me. I would have celebrated his death had I been allowed."

The knowledge hit Cora like a snowball in the middle of her forehead. "You're in love with Blake aren't you? That's how you know you didn't love your husband. Love is like nothing I've ever felt before and you know that feeling, too."

Nellie nodded and then quickly looked over her shoulder. "I do, but he doesn't and can't know it. Not until I'm sure he loves me, too."

"But you're expecting. Don't you think he loves you now?"

"I do, but he hasn't said the words to me."

"I understand. But I know that Asa loves me just by the way he treats me and also he's told me, so why can't I believe it? Why can't I just love him back?"

"Because you're scared. He's left you alone once and you're afraid he'll do it again."

Cora took a deep breath and then let it out. "I am. No matter what he tells me, I'm afraid he'll abandon me."

"Ladies," Blake entered the parlor followed by Asa. "We thought you might like some company this evening. I thought as long as Asa and Cora are here, they can stay for dinner and we can play Whist. What say you, ladies?"

"Oh, yes," Nellie took Cora's hands in hers. "Say you'll stay."

"Asa? Do you want to stay? I'd like to." She looked at Asa and wondered if he'd heard her state her fears when he came in and that was why he was suddenly quiet.

He looked at her and gave her a barely there smile. "Then that's what we'll do." He turned to Blake. "We'd love to stay. Thank you."

Blake clapped his hands and rubbed them together. "Get ready to lose, my friends. Nellie and I are a force to be reckoned with at Whist."

Asa laughed, but to Cora's ear the sound seemed forced.

"I'm sure we'll give you a run for your money," said Asa.

"Shall we get started?" Blake swept his

arm toward the door. "It's a couple of hours until dinner. I bet we can beat you a couple of times before the food is on the table. This way to the card room."

Cora hooked her arm through the crook of Nellie's. "Card room? Good grief, how big is this place?"

"Huge. Even after more than two months of being here, I'm still finding rooms I didn't know were there."

"Where are the kids? I haven't seen Henry or Violet yet."

"They are with Bertha at the park. She tries to take them every day. If not then they play in the back yard. Otis, our driver and James, who you know, put up a swing in the big oak tree back there. They did it on their own."

"That was very nice of them."

"It was. Blake didn't know about it until just recently, but he was happy they had installed it for the children."

They quickly reached the card room. Like all the other rooms in the house, a great mahogany door served as the entrance to the room. Inside there were four card tables set up. Each with upholstered wing back chairs on the four sides. The chair's upholstery was a solid mauve color and matched the background on the wallpaper. The dark burgundy drapes set off the walls, papered in a soft floral pattern with mauve background. The room was lovely and yet very masculine.

Their footsteps sounded across the wooden parquet floor. If it had been Cora's house she would have the room carpeted. The sound of people coming and going across the floor would be very distracting to the card players.

Blake led them to the table closest to the door. "Here we are. Take your seats and I'll ring for refreshments."

"Not too much, dear, just the essentials: tea, coffee, cookies. We don't want to get full before dinner. Cook is fixing her famous Beef Wellington tonight." Nellie turned to Asa. "Regardless of why you came, it is the perfect night to come over. You'll be so glad you agreed to stay for dinner."

Cora's mouth began to water. She'd had the dish before and fallen in love with the beef topped with liver pate and wrapped in light pastry dough, then baked until medium rare and served with a béarnaise sauce. Sometimes she thought she loved the sauce more than the meat.

"What are you smiling about?" asked Asa.

She hadn't realized she was. "I was thinking about dinner," she answered honestly. "Beef Wellington is probably my favorite dish."

Nellie squeezed Cora's hand. "See? You were meant to stop by today."

Blake rolled his eyes at his wife's comment. He took the cards setting on the table, shuffled them and dealt each of them a hand. "Let's play shall we?"

After dinner and another game of Whist, Cora couldn't stop the yawn that sneaked up.

"I'm so sorry. I seem to be tired. I think it's time to go."

"I'll have my driver take you back to Cora's shop. Would you like him to drop you at your hotel, Asa?"

"No, I'll see Cora settled then walk back to the hotel. The trip in the fresh air will do me good and it's only about eight blocks from Cora's place."

They said their goodnights to Blake and Nellie. When they got settled in the carriage, Cora sat across from Asa, rather than next to him as she usually did. That she loved him was the hardest part of all this. How could he love her back, when she'd put him through so very much? When she should have married him when he first came to San Francisco for her.

She looked out the window and pretended to be engrossed in the night view of the city.

"Are you glad we came?" Asa's voice boomed in the confined space of the coach, even though he'd spoken softly.

She turned toward him and nodded. "I had a wonderful time. It was good to just play cards and have dinner and not have to relive the...well you know."

"Yes, I know and I understand more than you think I do about how you're feeling."

"How can you?" She wanted to shout at him, her hands grabbed handfuls of her skirt. He couldn't understand the pain, the violation, only felt on the inside. She had a couple of bruises but nothing else that showed. "You've never been through—"

"Yes, I have." He was calm, his words spoken as though from far away. "How do you think I felt when they took my leg? I didn't have a choice. They took it while I was unconscious, which now, I'm very glad they did. If they hadn't cut the injured limb off, I probably would have died, or at best been confined to a chair or my bed. I wouldn't want to live like that."

"I'm sorry, I'm so sorry. I…" She covered her face with her hands and cried.

Asa was next to her in a flash, taking her in his arms and holding her.

"Shh, it's all right. You have nothing to be sorry for. What you went though is a horrible thing. You have every right to grieve for what you lost."

She shook her head. "But he didn't…I'm still…"

"I know he didn't take your virginity, but you did lose your innocence. You know now terrible, evil people are out there. Whereas before you may have thought that but you didn't have any experience with such people."

She gazed up at Asa. She saw no pity in his eyes, just understanding and that made her love him all the more and scared the hell out of her, too. What would she do if he left again? He said he wouldn't, and he'd done everything possible to prove his steadfastness but there was that niggling doubt in her mind. That doubt prevented her from completely trusting him with her heart.

"Cora. We're here, honey. What are you thinking so hard about?"

She shook her head to clear her thoughts. "What? Oh, we're here. No, nothing really."

He furrowed his eyebrows but didn't question her further.

Cora unlocked the door and led the way to her rooms above the shop.

"Come in Asa. We need to talk."

He cocked his eyebrow in question, but he followed her inside.

She closed the door behind him.

"Would you like some tea or coffee perhaps? I can make a pot."

"Tea is fine, thank you." He took off his hat and placed it on one of the pegs next to the door.

Cora went to the kitchen and bustled around lighting the stove and filling the kettle with water from the pump at the sink.

While the water heated, she got down two small plates from the cupboard and the homemade cookies off the top of the icebox. "Would you like a cookie?"

"Yes, please. Oatmeal cookies are my favorite."

She smiled. "I know."

"What would you like to talk about?"

"Us."

He sat up a little straighter.

"What about us?"

"These past months have been a whirlwind of activity and I've loved every minute I've spent with you."

"I hear a 'but' coming."

"But, I don't know if I want to get married. How can you still want to marry me, knowing what happened?"

Asa leaned across the table and took her hand in his. "What happened…is you were attacked. Do you think I care any less because you were assaulted? None of that was your fault. How can I make you believe it? What do I need to say?"

"I don't know. I only know that if I married you now, I wouldn't know if it was because I love you or because I want you to protect me or simply because you already know my reputation is tarnished."

"You're not tarnished." He paused and his voice dropped to a whisper. "What did you say?"

"You want to protect me?"

"No, before that. You said...you love me."

"I...I..." She couldn't deny it, but she hadn't realized she'd said those words. "It doesn't matter."

"What do you mean 'it doesn't matter'? Your proclamation makes all the difference in the world. If you love me, then together, we can do anything."

Cora shook her head. "I'd always wonder if you were marrying me out of pity. How can you not?"

Asa stood and pulled Cora into his arms. His lips slanted over hers in hungry passion. When he finally broke the kiss, he continued to hold her tight. "Does that feel like pity? I'll never pity you. I'm proud of you. You fought back and it saved you, Cora. Not me. You saved yourself."

"Me?" Surprise filled her.

"Yes. You. If you hadn't fought, the deed would have been done and you would have thought you didn't have any choice but to marry Harry, but you listen and listen well—I will love you and marry you, no matter what. Nothing you can do would make me stop loving you."

"How can you say that? How can you love me, knowing…" She couldn't say the words, afraid to voice the horror out loud, that it would become real…again. All she wanted was to forget.

"Knowing what?" He held her out at arm's length so he could see her face. "That you're the bravest woman I've ever met? That you are strong and can take care of yourself when you need to? But I don't want you to need to anymore. I want you to let me take care of you. Marry me, Cora. Now, today. Let's not wait any longer."

Her heart overflowed with warmth from deep down inside. "Asa, I do love you and I want to marry you, but are you sure—"

His lips silenced her.

Finally, she stopped arguing and melted into him.

CHAPTER 12

They stayed on the sofa and kissed and held each other confident in the knowledge they possessed enough love to get them through the hard times ahead.

Cora rested her head on his chest. Asa held her with both arms wrapped around her as though he was afraid to lose her.

"We can't get married today, it's already night and the courthouse is closed." Now that Cora was sure she loved him, she wanted to get married as soon as possible. "But tomorrow, first thing, we'll go get Blake and Nellie, and then get ourselves to the first available judge."

"I happen to know that Blake knows a judge who would be available for him, if we just let him know."

She eased away enough to stare. "You mean go back there now and tell them?"

He chuckled. "No, tomorrow is soon enough."

"Asa, are you sure…"

He lifted her chin and gazed into her eyes. "Cora. I swear, I love you more than anything, and every time you ask me I'll just kiss you, so you can ask me all you want."

She smiled and looked down at their clasped hands. "Asa?"

"Hmm?"

"Do you love—"

He lifted her face up and claimed her lips. Each kiss was better than the last and this one was no exception. He kissed her until she was breathless and so was he.

"Oh, Asa. I do love you so."

"I know."

She felt the thundering of his heart and knew hers pounded just as hard.

"Don't leave me, tonight," she whispered.

He squeezed her. "I'm not going anywhere. I won't let you out of my sight."

"Love me, tonight. I know we aren't married yet, but we will be tomorrow and—

" So full of love for Asa, she wanted to show him. Prove her love for him.

Shaking his head, Asa placed two fingers gently over her lips. "I won't make you mine until we're married. I know you want that, want to feel alive and whole, but we can wait. Our love can wait until we are well and truly married."

"But—" Disappointed, yet proud that he would honor her this way, she acquiesced to his wishes.

"No buts. I'll stay tonight and hold you in my arms all night, but tomorrow we will be husband and wife."

She smiled. "Being held by you is all I really need right now. But then, you know that, don't you?"

He settled her against his shoulder. "I know. Being held, being safe is what you need and what I can provide you tonight."

"I love you, Asa."

"I love you, Cora. Always have and always will."

*****

The next day Cora dressed in the new purple silk gown she'd designed and sewn. She was going to wear the pink satin she'd made when she was to marry Asa before, but that was then. This was now and the purple dress was now, too. It fit her like a glove and accented her curves. She put on her purple silk hat she'd had made to match the gown. It had a wide brim and was perfect for a Sunday outing or in this case, a wedding. She walked out of the bedroom. Asa was at the stove pouring a cup of coffee.

He turned when she entered and whistled. "You look spectacular. We have to stop by the hotel and let me change my clothes before we go to Blake and Nellie's."

"Well let's get going. Put the damper on the stove and swallow that coffee."

"To heck with the coffee." He closed off the burner and set the coffee cup in the sink. Then he held out his arm. "Miss Jones?"

Feeling so happy, Cora took his arm. "Mr. Woods"

They laughed, walked down the stairs and out of the shop, caught the first cab they saw and went to Asa's hotel. She waited in the lobby while he went to change.

When he returned, he'd changed into his black suit with black vest and tie. His shirt was starched and crisp white, against which his tan skin stood in stark contrast. He was so handsome, her Asa.

Smiling, he turned to face her. "Are you ready?"

She beamed. "Am I ever? I can barely wait to be your wife."

They locked arms, walked out of the hotel and to a waiting cab which took them to Blake and Nellie's.

Asa helped Cora out of the carriage and together they walked up the brick path to the door. He knocked twice before the door opened on James.

"Good morning, Mr. Woods and Miss Jones. Please come in. The Malone's are in the dining room. I'll show you the way."

Cora walked through the dining room door first, fighting back a smile at her friends' surprised expression.

"Cora." Nellie dropped her toast on her plate and got up to greet them. "And Asa, what are you two doing here this morning?" She gave Cora a kiss on the cheek.

"It's sort of obvious, my dear," said Blake. "They are both dressed in their Sunday best and it's only Friday. They are getting married and want us to join them."

"That's exactly right." Asa closed his hand around Cora's and they followed Nellie to the table. They sat in the two chairs next to her. "We thought you two could stand up for us and we hoped you knew a judge that might be willing to perform the ceremony on short notice."

With a quick nod, Blake put his napkin on his plate. "As a matter of fact I do. Give Nellie and me a bit to get ready."

Only after Blake had said it did Cora realize they were both in their dressing gowns.

"Oh, my stars. I'm so sorry. I hadn't realized just how early it is. Asa and I are so excited…"

"Nonsense. It's not a problem." Nellie rose from the table. "Give us a few minutes. Have some breakfast while you wait, or at least a cup of coffee."

Cora shook her head. "I don't think I could eat a thing, but maybe a cup of tea, if it's no trouble."

"James, please bring Miss Jones some tea."

"Yes, Madam."

He went to the sideboard and filled a cup from the teapot sitting there.

"Your tea, Miss." He put the full teacup in front of Cora.

"Would you care for some tea or coffee,

sir?" he asked Asa.

"Coffee, please."

James brought the coffee and then retreated to his station by the sidebar.

Cora sipped at her tea, and then set the cup on the saucer. "I'm too excited and nervous to drink tea."

Asa squeezed her hand and comforted her. "We'll be there soon and you'll be my wife."

She placed two fingers against his lips and grinned. "You'll be my husband and you can't get out of it now."

"Ah, here we are." Nellie entered wearing a forest green dress. "I hope you don't mind if the children come."

"Cora." Violet ran at her.

Cora stood, caught her and gave her a big hug. "Of course, I don't mind." She looked over at Henry who was being more circumspect, but who, she could tell, wanted to run to her arms just like Violet did.

She held her arms wide. "Henry."

He walked to her and wrapped his arms around her waist. "Cora, I've missed you so much."

"I've missed you too, sweetheart. I can't believe how big you've gotten in just a couple of months." She held him at arm's length and looked down at his pants. "Blake must be taking you to his tailor, your pants don't need letting down."

Henry nodded. "He does, twice so far, and we've ordered pants both times. He says I'm growing like a weed."

"And he would be right."

"Are we all ready?" Blake drew on his black driving gloves.

Answers in the affirmative came from everyone.

"Then let's get this party started." Blake led everyone out to the waiting carriage.

After a short trip to the courthouse, they disembarked the coach and entered the building. Blake led the way to Judge Homer Clemmons' office. He knocked on the door and then entered. The rest of them followed.

"Blake Malone to see Judge Clemmons," he said to the young man sitting at the desk outside the judge's chambers.

"Yes, sir, Mr. Malone. Please be seated, ladies." He pointed at the two chairs against the wall.

Nellie sat. "Might as well be comfortable."

"I don't think I could sit still. I'm so nervous." Cora paced in front of Nellie, her heart beating hard. She was almost Mrs. Asa Woods.

Violet kept up with Cora step for step.

Henry sat next to his mother.

Blake chuckled. "Asa, will you hold her hand and keep her still?"

"I'd have an easier time if I just paced with her like Violet is."

The young man reentered the room. "The judge will see you now. This way, please."

They followed him into the chambers.

Behind a large wooden desk sat an equally large man with white hair and full beard of silver whiskers. He looked up as they all came in and then he stood. "Blake, my boy, how are you? Ah, and the sweet Nellie. Are you keeping my boy in line?"

"I do my best, Judge." Nellie smiled.

"Good. Good. Now, I would guess since there are four of you and these two youngsters, all looking like you're headed either to church or the opera that we are to have another wedding. Am I right?"

"Yes, sir, Homer. Right you are." Blake grabbed Asa by the arm and brought him forward. "These are our friends, Asa Woods and Cora Jones. They want, no, make that they *need* to get married before they do something they regret."

"Oh, ho. I guess we'd better take care of this right away. I don't suppose you have a license."

Asa shook his head then turned and stared at Cora. "No, sir. I'm afraid we don't."

"Not to worry. Norman will take care of it. Norman!" Judge Clemmons bellowed.

"Yes, sir," said the young man from the doorway.

"Prepare a marriage license for these two. Mr. Asa Woods and Miss Cora Jones. We're having a wedding."

"Yes, sir. Right away, sir."

The judge hooked his hands over his round belly. "There see. All taken care of. Now, let me find my glasses and the good book and we'll be ready to start."

Several minutes passed while the judge looked for his glasses. Turned out they were in his jacket pocket.

"All right now. You two," he pointed as Asa and Cora. "Come stand in front of me. Asa on my left and Cora on my right. Nellie you stand beside Cora and Blake beside Asa. Good. Good."

Cora looked up at Asa and smiled. It was happening, really happening. She was marrying her Asa. Her love.

He grinned back at her. "You ready?"

She nodded, her throat tight. "Yes. You?"

"Always."

"What 'bout me?" Violet crossed her arms over her little chest and frowned, looking for all the world like she was going to cry.

"Here, baby girl." Cora held out her hand. "You stand with me. "

Violet smiled and stepped to the front of the group with Cora.

"Young man," said the judge to Henry. "You stand next to Blake."

"Yes, sir." Henry move next to Blake and put his hands behind his back.

"Now." The judge looked over all of them. "I think we are ready. We are gathered here in front of these witnesses..."

Cora looked up at Asa, who smiled down at her. She couldn't believe she was finally marrying Asa. Her friend Asa. Her love. Asa. Through her fog of happiness, she became aware of the judge's words again.

"Do you Asa Woods, take this woman, Cora Jones to be your lawful wedded wife? To have and to hold, for richer or poorer, through sickness and health for all the days you shall live from this day forward?"

After a long look into her eyes, Asa squeezed her hand. "I do."

"You may place the ring on her finger."

Asa took her hand and place the ring on her third finger. "With this ring, I thee wed," he repeated after the judge.

Judge Clemmons gazed at her. "Do you have a ring, young woman?"

Ring! I don't have a ring. Wait, yes I do.

"Yes, sir, just a moment." Cora reached up and took the chain from around her neck and slid a heavy gold ring off of it. She took Asa's hand and placed the band on his finger. "It was my daddy's."

Asa nodded. "I know. I recognize it."

"With this ring I thee wed." The ring was a little big and would have to be sized, but for now it was perfect.

"By the power vested in me by the State of California and the City of San Francisco, I now pronounce you man and wife. You may kiss the bride."

Asa place the palms of his hands on her face. "I love you Cora Woods." His lips met hers.

Rather than the chaste kiss she was expecting, he drank from her, sipped her sweetness and returned his own.

Blake started clapping and Nellie joined in. Of course, Violet couldn't let the grownups do anything she didn't so she started clapping, too as did Henry.

Asa lifted his head, wrapped his arm around Cora's waist and turned to face everyone. "Thank you for helping us and sharing our joy. Let's go to the Golden State Hotel and celebrate. Cora and I have made some wonderful memories and have had delightful meals there. You wouldn't know by looking at the place, but they have a world class chef."

CHAPTER 13

After a wonderful meal, Asa and Cora bid goodbye to Blake, Nellie and their family.

"Let's go back to my apartment." She was anxious to make love to her handsome husband. To start their new life together.

"We're going to spend our first night together here, not at your apartment."

"But why?"

"This hotel holds no bad memories of any kind and I want our first time together to be special."

"That's exactly why I want to go home. You and I will live there." She smiled and nestled into his side as they walked up the stairs to his room. "I want to build good memories. I want to have so many good memories that I don't remember the bad. So pack your bags, you're moving home."

Asa took a deep breath and let it out. "You make good sense. Let me get my things and we'll be off."

He packed only what he'd need tomorrow. They would come back then to pack up the rest of his belongings and check him out of the hotel.

They walked the few blocks to Creations by Cora. She looked at the window in the door. She'd replaced the broken one but sometimes she wondered if she shouldn't have left it so she would never forget. No. She wouldn't think like that. She shook her head to clear her mind unlocked and opened the door, and after he was through, locked it again.

Once upstairs, Cora led him to the bedroom and moved her clothes in the closet to make room for his.

"You'll have to buy more clothes."

"I'll just send for them. Garrett can bring them when he and the rest of the staff come out."

She stopped and turned to face him. "Staff?"

"Cora, I haven't had a chance to tell you. Aunt Charlotte died and left me everything.

I'm very wealthy now, with a large mansion and a seven-member staff. I intend to build a home for us in the same area that Blake and Nellie live. Won't you like that?"

"Wealthy?" She sat down on the bed, suddenly overwhelmed. "We've never been wealthy. Either of us."

"I know." He smiled wide. "But it's easy to get used to."

She turned to him and asked sharply. "What about my shop? If you're rich you won't want a wife to work."

"Why not? Your shop and designing clothes, makes you happy and whatever makes you happy, I'm all for." He went over and sat beside her. "You are at your best when you're creating and helping women look good. The interaction with the customers is what you love and I don't want to change you."

Cora looked up at him with tears in her eyes. "Thank you. Thank you for knowing me. We still have lots to learn about each other but this is a huge step in the right direction."

"Are you done putting away my clothes and being surprised by our wealth? Because I'd really like to get to know you better...with all your clothes off."

She felt herself blush to the tips of her toes and knew she was just scarlet.

Cora wrapped her hand around his neck and brought his lips to meet hers. Before they kissed, she whispered, "I'd very much like to make love to you now."

He kissed her, slipping his hands between them and began unbuttoning her dress.

She pulled away and stood. "Let me." Finishing what he started, she unbuttoned the dress, slipped it off her shoulders and let it fall in a heap on the floor. She followed that with her corset and pantaloons, leaving only her chemise. "Now you. I want you naked."

Asa took off his clothes down to his under drawers and was about to take off his leg when she stopped him.

"Let me." She opened the metal clamp on his thigh and gently pulled off the wooden leg. Then she rubbed where the clamp had been, kneading and pressing, releasing the muscles confined for so long under the clamp that held the wooden leg on to his thigh. She knew it helped to rub her leg after having a cramp and thought the rubbing would help him to feel better too.

"That feels wonderful."

She gazed up at him, only love in her eyes. "I'm glad."

He lay back on the bed. "Take off your chemise. I want to look at you."

"Only if you take off your drawers."

"Deal. Together."

She shed her garment as he did his. He was ready for her, his member standing straight up and proud. But he was anxious, determined not to hurt her any more than necessary.

"God, you're beautiful."

She blushed. "Do you really think so?" She smoothed her hands over her hips. "You don't think I'm…fat?"

"You are perfect. Come here and lie with me."

He turned himself so he was lying on the bed with his head on the pillow. His leg still throbbed but it was so much better since Cora had rubbed his thigh. That was the nicest thing anyone had ever done for him.

She lay beside him, her body as stiff as a board.

He almost laughed, but this was her first time and she was scared.

Asa leaned up on one elbow. As much as he wanted to just plunge into his little wife, he wanted her to enjoy it as much as possible. This first time would be uncomfortable, but he'd do everything he could to alleviate the discomfort.

He chuckled. He couldn't help it. Cora laid there, arms at her sides, eyes closed and rigid enough to iron clothes on. "Cora?"

"Hmm."

"Open your eyes and look at me."

She did and when she saw him smiling, she smiled, too.

"Are you scared, sweetheart?"

She shook her head, but said "Yes."

Knowing he needed to be gentle, he took his free hand and began making lazy circles on her stomach, then up and around each breast.

She took a deep breath and relaxed a little.

He played with her nipples, squeezing them between his thumb and forefinger. Next, in his seduction of his wife, he took one of her beautiful pale, pink nipples in his mouth and suckled her.

"Asa! Dear God." She came up off the bed, pushing her breast more firmly into his mouth.

He chuckled. She was so responsive, his little bride. "Like that do you?"

Through shallower breathing, she said, "Yes."

"Cora, do you believe that I'll do my best not to hurt you?"

She nodded.

"And that I'll give you as much pleasure as humanly possible."

She cocked an eyebrow. "Pleasure? Really? Before mother died, she told me the marriage bed is something to be endured not enjoyed."

"Your mother was wrong. Making love is beautiful and if done right the most pleasurable of endeavors."

She cocked her head and looked at him, her mouth a straight line.

"Really, just keep an open mind and let yourself feel. That's all, just feel."

Cora closed her eyes for just a moment and then nodded. "I'll try."

Asa kissed her lips then moved to her jaw and down her neck. He knew he was making progress when she turned her head to give him greater access to the lily white column of her neck. He smiled.

Cora sucked in a breath through clenched teeth. She loved it when Asa kissed her, especially when he trailed little kisses along her neck and behind her ear. Sometimes he'd follow them with his tongue and send shivers up and down her spine.

He moved lower and took a nipple into his mouth and suckled. She couldn't help but gasp. Never in her life had she felt anything so wonderful. Her body came alive and she wanted more.

Asa seemed to know what she needed. With his hand he tweaked her other nipple, and the feelings in her groin made her clutch the bed sheets in her hands. He took his other hand and ran it down her body over her ribs and on to her mound where he pressed hard. Then he moved his hand in circles and Cora thought she would come off the bed, so intense was the pleasure.

She panted and rolled her head from side to side. "Please, Asa." Then he was there with his mouth, moving his tongue around and over her. When he pressed a finger inside of her, she shattered.

"Oh, God, Asa." Her body moved on its own without thought. The feelings he wrought from her were unlike anything she'd felt before and she loved them, wanted to feel more. Wanted to feel like this forever.

He grinned. "We made the right decision to come back here otherwise you'd have awakened the entire hotel." Then Asa moved up her body and positioned his hard shaft at her opening. "I've prepared you as best I can, my love. I'm sorry for any discomfort I cause you."

He pressed into her a short way and back out, again and again, a little farther each time. Then he slammed into her and through her maidenhead, splitting the barrier and sending a shaft of pain through her.

She gasped and tried to push him off her.

"Be still, Cora. Just a minute." The words sounded ripped from him like they took his very last effort to say.

She took a deep breath and stilled herself. As she did the sting subsided and she was left with a feeling of fullness that was not unpleasant.

"Are…you…better?"

She nodded and he kissed her long and hard as he began to move within her. Slowly at first and then faster and faster, until he groaned and collapsed against her holding her tight. He buried his face in the crook of her neck, breathing deeply.

Cora clasped him to her and rubbed his back.

"You are amazing," he said when he rolled to his side. He pulled her to him and spooned with her. "I love you, Cora."

She felt nothing but joy. She and Asa were one. One being, one life. The best of each other joined together. Forever.

"I love you, too."

EPILOGUE

July 1879

Cora sat on the porch swing with Asa. They often sat there in the evenings. Today was Sunday and they'd just finished a dinner of fried chicken, mashed potatoes and gravy, fresh greens from the garden and peach cobbler for dessert. Cook was from Atlanta and delighted in serving dishes she'd grown up with. Not that Cora minded, she loved it.

They watched Asa Jr., almost eleven, play on the grass with his brother, Charles, nine. They were trying to fly a kite but the wind kept sending it spiraling to the ground.

Their six-year-old twin girls, Sara and Charlotte, demonstrated to their little sister Maggie, three, how to make mud pies. Their clothes would never be the same. She was glad she'd insisted they change into play clothes as soon as they got home from church.

Baby Lawrence, they called him Larry, slept peacefully in the rocking bassinet Asa built. Cora had just weaned him. At ten months he was eating most foods if she cut them up small enough and mashed potatoes were his favorite.

"Did you ever think we could be this happy?" She rubbed Asa's thigh as she always did when then sat together and as she did every night after he removed his artificial leg.

His arm rested around her shoulders. He took her hand in his free one and looked down at her wedding ring. The plain gold band now had a sparkling blue sapphire solitaire ring next to it on her finger. "I dreamed about it the entire time I was in the hospital. I dreamed how our life could have been if I'd been whole. I never thought I'd be this content while missing my leg. You proved me wrong. These past twelve years have been the happiest of my life."

"Mine too. Do you ever think about the time we reunited?"

"Only that I'm so glad I arrived here in

San Francisco before you did. If I hadn't you might have married Harry and I don't want to think about what might have happened then."

"I try not to think about it, but sometimes, especially when I'm so happy and so thankful, those memories sneak in."

"Well just think of our children and how wonderful our family is." He squeezed her shoulder. "And those thoughts will go away."

"Oh, I do and they do but I can't seem to completely forget. Maybe that's why I appreciate what we have together so very much."

"Me, too. We've accomplished what most people can't because Aunt Charlotte left me the wherewithal to make our life easier."

"Well, Creations by Cora helped, too. The shop has become very successful."

"Thanks in no small part to its creator." He leaned down and kissed the top of her head. "If not for your designs, the store would be just that, another store. You make it special, just as you make our family special."

"Speaking of family..." Cora looked

down and played with the ties to the bonnet lying in her lap.

"Yes," she heard the question in his voice.

"What would you think of having more children?"

"You know I love our children. If you want more than we'll do our best to have more."

"We've already been doing our best, I'm expecting again."

Asa squeezed her shoulder. "You don't sound too happy about that."

"I'm just a little worried. Larry is only ten months old. A new baby will be like having twins again. Two in diapers."

He nodded. "That's true, but I'll help you and we have Maudie to help with the children. She'll be thrilled to have a new baby. You know how she is. She's spoiled every one of our children, I don't see any reason to stop her now. The only thing I worry about is you. Are you sure you're up to having another baby?"

Cora smiled "It's kind of too late to ask that question."

"We'll start using protection. I can prevent you getting pregnant."

"No, I think we'll have all the children the good Lord chooses for us to have."

"Whatever makes you happy my love."

He took his index finger and placed it gently on her jaw, and turned her head to him. Then he slanted his lips over hers in a kiss both tender and fierce. His tongue pressed against her lips and she let him in savoring the taste of him. Coffee and peach cobbler with clotted cream. Then he pulled back and squeezed her tight to him.

"I love you, Cora Woods. You gave me back my life. You and the children are everything to me."

"As you and they are to me." She reached up and cupped his jaw. His whiskers were already growing in and were rough against her palm. "My life literally started over when we married. I'm so glad you came after me. I love you, Asa."

They sat together, watching the children, content, appreciating each other and simply thankful for the life they had. Cora never forgot what could have happened and was grateful everyday for her family and especially for her Asa.

Her perfect man.

ABOUT THE AUTHOR

Cynthia Woolf is the award winning and best-selling author of twelve historical western romance books and two short stories with more books on the way. She was born in Denver, Colorado and raised in the mountains west of Golden. She spent her early years running wild around the mountain side with her friends.

Their closest neighbor was about one quarter of a mile away, so her little brother was her playmate and her best friend. That fierce friendship lasted until his death in 2006.

Cynthia was and is an avid reader. Her mother was a librarian and brought new books home each week. This is where young Cynthia first got the storytelling bug. She wrote her first story at the age of ten. A romance about a little boy she liked at the time.

Cynthia loves writing and reading romance. Her first western romance Tame A Wild Heart, was inspired by the story her mother told her of meeting Cynthia's father on a ranch in Creede, Colorado. Although Tame A Wild Heart takes place in Creede that is the only similarity between the stories. Her father was a cowboy not a bounty hunter and her mother was a nursemaid (called a nanny now) not the ranch owner.

Cynthia credits her wonderfully supportive husband Jim and the great friends she's made at CRW for saving her sanity and allowing her to explore her creativity.

TITLES AVAILABLE

NELLIE – The Brides of San Francisco 1
ANNIE – The Brides of San Francisco 2
CORA – The Brides of San Francisco 3
REDEEMED BY A REBEL (Book 1, Destiny in Deadwood series)
HEALED BY A HEART (Book 2, Destiny in Deadwood series)
SEDUCED BY A SINNER (Book 3, Destiny in Deadwood series)
CAPITAL BRIDE (Book 1, Matchmaker & Co. series)
HEIRESS BRIDE (Book 2, Matchmaker & Co. series)
FIERY BRIDE (Book 3, Matchmaker & Co. series)
TAME A WILD HEART (Book 1, Tame series)
TAME A WILD WIND (Book 2, Tame series)
TAME A WILD BRIDE (Book 3, Tame series)
TAME A SUMMER HEART (short story, Tame series)

WEBSITE – www.cynthiawoolf.com

NEWSLETTER - http://bit.ly/1qBWhFQ

Made in the USA
Lexington, KY
16 May 2015